Linda Joy Singleton lives in northern California and often has strange encounters with playful cats, demanding dogs, and even pigs and horses. She has two grown children and a wonderfully supportive husband who loves to travel with her in search of unusual stories.

Linda Joy Singleton is the author of more than twenty-five books.

Visit Linda and other Llewellyn authors on the Web at:

teen.llewellyn.com

# Sea Switch

## Linda Joy Singleton

Llewellyn Publications
Woodbury, Minnesota

FIRST EDITION
First printing, 2005

Cover design by Ellen L. Dahl
Cover illustration © 2004 by Mike Harper/Artworks
Editing by Megan Atwood and Rhiannon Ross
Interior illustration by Ellen L. Dahl
Series book design by Andrew Karre

Llewellyn is a registered trademark of Llewellyn Worldwide, Ltd.


**Library of Congress Cataloging-in-Publication Data (Pending)**
ISBN: 0-7387-0712-0

Llewellyn Publications
A Division of Llewellyn Worldwide, Ltd.
2143 Wooddale Drive, Dept. 0-7387-0712-0
Woodbury, MN 55125-2989, U.S.A.
www.llewellyn.com

Printed in the United States of America

## Also from Linda Joy Singleton

*To my niece,*
*Jillian Rose Emburg*

# Contents

## chapter one

# Sister Secrets

When I saw my little sister tiptoe out of our room carrying her hamster cage, I knew she was up to something. Something sneaky.

What was it with Amber anyway? Why couldn't she sleep like a normal kid? I mean, it was 6:09 in the morning! The alarm wouldn't go off for another 51 minutes, and then my family would rush around like crazy getting ready for a long drive to Oregon.

So where was Amber taking Mama Hamster and the four babies? Even for my animal-obsessed sister that was weird.

1

And *highly* suspicious.

Snapping on my bedside light, I sat up and tried to figure this out.

*Amber + pets + trip = ?* I mentally calculated. Then I nearly fell out of bed as the most obvious answer smacked me like a concrete pillow.

*Not again!* I thought with a groan. Amber had this totally annoying habit of sneaking pets on trips. Last month she smuggled her pet duck Dribble on a campout. Next she took an alien pet to a mountain resort. Fortunately our parents never found out—but keeping a dancing, hair-eating alien a secret nearly drove me crazy! Now, with only a few hours until we left for an Oregon beach vacation, my animal-obsessed sister was up to her usual tricks.

*Well she's not getting away with it!* I vowed, slinging off my covers. *This time I'll make sure she doesn't smuggle any pets!*

I tossed on a robe and scooted into fuzzy pink slippers. Then I raced out of my room. A door squeaked from the kitchen, and I guessed that Amber was cutting through the kitchen into the garage. I started in that direction, then changed my mind. The squeaky door would give me away, and I wanted the element of surprise. So I headed outside, circling around to the side garage door.

Nearing the garage, I heard voices. Stealthily, I twisted the knob and peeked past boxes, bikes, and old furniture until I saw my sister talking to a small girl with black hair poking out in four curly ponytails. Six-year-old Olivia lived next door and was so shy she hardly ever talked, or maybe she didn't say much because she was always chewing a big wad of gum. She and Amber became friends last year when Amber organized a pet pageant and Olivia's calico cat Prissy won first place in the "Longest Tail" category.

"Look how their whiskers wiggle! They're so cute!" Olivia exclaimed, and even with her back turned toward me, I knew she was admiring the baby hamsters.

"You want one?" Amber offered, which surprised me because Amber never gave away her pets. She still hadn't forgiven me for giving away her alien

3

pet even though I explained that Jennifer would be happier with other magical beings. Her side of our bedroom was like a small zoo, with an aquarium, a terrarium, and a hamster hotel. And our family dog Honey shared the backyard with Amber's rabbit cage and duck pond.

"Oh, yes! I can't wait to have my own!" Olivia replied with an enthusiastic smack of her gum. "I really, really love them so much."

"Me, too. Wanna trade now?" Amber asked.

Olivia nodded enthusiastically.

"Which one?"

"The white baby and the brown baby."

"But that's two!" my sister shook her head. "I said just one."

"Well I want two," Olivia said stubbornly. "It's only fair."

"Is not!"

"Is too. My trade is super good. You're gonna get—" Olivia bent over the hamster cage and spoke so softly I could only understand some of her words. "Add water and grow . . . babies . . . three eyes."

4

*Grow babies?* I puzzled. Plants grew when you added water. Not babies. And what kind of pet had three eyes? I must have heard wrong.

Someone tapped my shoulder. "Hey, Cassie!"

Startled, I whirled around and shrieked, "Rosalie!" I scowled at my best friend. "What are you doing here?"

"What do you think?" Her black eyes sparkled as she held up her bulging duffel bag. She wore her favorite red sneakers and a *Kings Rule* T-shirt over silky red shorts. "I'm all packed and ready for our big trip. I know I'm early, but I couldn't wait to get here. Is that okay?"

"Yeah, but your timing stinks." I turned around to look into the garage. Just as I feared—Amber and Olivia were gone. Darn! They must have heard my shriek and high-tailed it through the kitchen door.

"What's so interesting in the garage?" Rosalie peered over my shoulder, her thick black braid slapping against me.

"Nothing anymore." I kicked the door shut. "I'll tell you while we load your bag. Come on." As we headed to my family's green Aerostar van, I explained about Amber, Olivia, and the baby hamsters.

"No way!" Rosalie exclaimed. "Amber never gives away her pets."

"She didn't *give* them away. She traded."

"For what?"

"I don't know. What kind of pet has three eyes?"

"A freak of nature like the two-headed snake I saw on TV. We'll see lots of weird stuff like that at the Ripley Museum."

"If we make it there without Amber causing problems," I said ominously. "When she smuggled her duck on our campout, Mom almost canceled the whole trip."

"Your parents won't cancel," Rosalie insisted, tilting her *Monarchs* cap to block out the bright morning sun. Never Give Up was her motto, especially when she played sports. Even when she lost a game, she never lost her optimistic attitude.

"I hope you're right," I said with an uneasy glance at the garage.

"Absolutely." She flashed a grin that showed off the green-tinted braces. "Besides, didn't you say your mom has to go to some beach meeting in Oregon?"

"Yeah. For her Happy Planet Club," I explained, stopping at the rear of the van. "They're taking part in a big beach clean up. And Dad has stuff to do for his TV show."

"See? Your parents won't cancel our trip. Amber could pack an elephant and we'd still go."

"But we'd need a much bigger car."

"Nah." She grinned. "Elephants come with their own trunks."

I groaned at her pun as I popped open the van's back door. It was jam-packed with suitcases, folding chairs, blankets, beach towels, and an ice chest. With creative pushing and shoving, we squeezed Rosalie's duffel bag beside my brother Lucas's black leather suitcase.

"While your parents are busy," Rosalie added, "we'll have a blast doing the three S's."

"Three S's?" I raised my brows.

She held up three fingers. "Swimming, shopping, and sightseeing."

"I can't wait!" Slamming the door shut, I grinned. I'd hardly had time to unpack my suitcase from our recent trip to Mt. Shasta, and here we were going away again. Unbelievable! When I started sixth grade in September, I'd have plenty to write about under the topic of "My Summer Vacation."

Of course, I didn't dare write about what *really* happened. Who would believe that I'd hung out on a spaceship with a silver-skinned alien or played magical games in a hidden underground community? My brother Lucas had shared in the magic, so he was the only other human who knew the truth.

But that was going to change. Soon.

I'd made a HUGE decision. I was going to tell Rosalie about aliens and magic because best friends should share everything. A relaxing, ordinary trip to the beach was the perfect place to reveal my out-of-this-world secrets.

So nothing weird was allowed on this trip—especially something weird with three eyeballs.

## chapter two

# Dead Magic

An hour later everyone was gathered in the dining room for a quick breakfast of wheat germ cinnamon buns and kiwi juice. As I chewed, I watched Amber closely across the table. She looked angelic with golden hair and innocent blue eyes. But I didn't trust her. If trouble came packaged, it would be labeled "Amber."

Standing up, I told my parents I'd just remembered something I needed to pack. Instead of heading for my room, I whizzed back to the van and searched Amber's zoo-patterned suitcase. Twice. But I only found T-shirts, jeans, socks, coloring books, crayons, books, and puzzles.

*Nothing alive,* I discovered. *The closest thing to a pet is a saggy stuffed bear. And he won't cause any problems.*

Relieved, I headed back for the house. Since I'd made the excuse of getting something from my room, I went there to double-check the packing list I'd posted on my bulletin board. For a short trip, this was a looong list. I'd packed snacks (red licorice for Rosalie, chocolate raisins for me), the latest fantasy book by Eva Ibbotson, a *World Traveler* magazine, a deck of cards, and two new Madlib games.

Now, as I studied the list, I thought of one more thing I should take. A top-secret, out-of-this-world object I'd tucked away in the back of my closet.

I had two of these. The first was a zillofax—like a backpack for aliens. It was larger than my suitcase and recycled by aliens from garbage humans dumped in space. It wasn't magical, but had been owned by my alien friend Zee.

The object hidden in the dark pit of my closet was much smaller . . . and way more mysterious. I called it my "crystal globe." When Lucas and I visited a secret community under Mount Shasta, the globe glittered with magic. It showed me a vision of Rosalie so real I could hear what she was saying hundreds of miles away. When Lucas looked inside, he glimpsed himself in the future as a Broadway star.

Unfortunately the magic died when I returned to my own world.

Yet when light reflected on its prisms, I sensed that it still held power. Even without magic, it sparkled like a priceless jewel. So I planned to show it to Rosalie when we had our serious talk. I hoped it would help convince her that my magical adventures were real. Then Rosalie would know all of my secrets.

But would she believe me?

## chapter three

# Splish Splash

A short time later, we were on the road. Yahoo! Oregon here we come!

I was settled into the van beside Rosalie. In the seat behind us, Amber flipped through a *Highlights* magazine while my brother Lucas studied a script for his drama class production of *Peter Pan* (he had the role of the crocodile). In the front seat, my dad drove while Mom consulted a map.

Sounds like a nice, normal family vacation, right? Well, I hoped so. But when your last name was Strange, anything could happen. And lately it had all been happening to me. I used to think I was the only average person in my unusual family. Boy had I been wrong! I was like a magnet attracting weird stuff.

But with Rosalie along for this trip, everything would be perfect. She was the most normal person I knew, except for her obsession with sports. Track, swimming, basketball, soccer, volleyball . . . you name it, Rosalie played it. She even had a collection of sport caps signed by famous athletes.

Our trip started off with excited conversation. But after an hour of driving, boredom attacked. Rosalie and I were like zombies watching out the window, seeing only miles and miles of flat, yellow-brown nothing fields. Brain numbing! I yawned, and Rosalie—who got antsy sitting for too long—squirmed in her seatbelt. Fortunately I'd planned for such a dire predicament and pulled out my emergency stash of games. Brain-Aid, I called it.

"Give me a noun, an adjective, and a body part," Rosalie said, flipping open to a page of *Monster Madlibs*.

"Frog, funny, and nose," I told her.

She asked for more words and I answered off the top of my head, words like fungus, toenail, and booger. Rosalie giggled as she scribbled down my answers. "This is the best yet," she said. "Wait till you hear."

"Well stop laughing and read already."

"Okay, okay." She sniffled and wiped her eyes. "It's called *Monster Love*. It starts off: Cassie put a frog on her funny nose and entered Frankenstein's toilet." Rosalie burst into giggles. I threatened to take it away from her if she didn't compose herself. Of course, by the time she finished reading, we were both laughing so much Lucas yelled that we were disturbing him.

Naturally, I told him to shove it and mind his own business. He called me a really rude name, so Rosalie rushed to my defense by threatening to give him a wedgie. At this point, Mom turned around with some threats. No argument was worth being grounded to a hotel room on our vacation.

So we stopped arguing.

It felt like being in a time warp—driving for miles and hours, climbing higher into lush green mountains. When our ears got all funny because of the altitude change, Mom passed out spearmint gum. Chewing made my ears pop and feel normal again. The sounds of smacking gum made me think of Olivia and I glanced suspiciously at Amber. What had she traded and where was it now?

When we reached the hotel in Roseburg, I forgot all about Amber when I heard there was an indoor pool and a hot tub. Woo hoo! Splash down here I come!

Rosalie and I didn't waste time unpacking. We grabbed our swimsuits and towels. "Last one to the pool is a slimy frog!" she shouted.

"Get ready for some warts," I teased back as I zipped around her. When we burst into the recreation room, Lucas was already splashing in the deep end of the pool.

"Your brother got here first. Guess we're both frogs," Rosalie joked.

"Hurry into the pool before we croak." I ran fast and then leaped high, coming down SPLASH! and swamping my brother. Rosalie giggled, splashing down next to me, and we shared a look that clearly meant "Frogs Unite!"

After playing freeze tag and Marco Polo in the pool for a while, we tried out the hot tub. It was . . . well . . . hot! In a cool, fantastic, forget-your-problems way. Bubbles erupted from underwater jets and frothy foam tickled my face. I leaned back against a powerful jet and sank into bliss.

My mind wandered. I imagined we were soaking in the sun on the beach with soft waves lapping against sand. A sense of peace flowed over me and I was floating, adrift in warm waves. I wondered if this was how it felt to be a fish. Underwater there were no rules or homework or chores. Only peaceful swimming and total freedom. Life as a fish would be cool—as long as you avoided sharp hooks.

I was mentally swimming in Australia's Barrier Reef when the timer dinged and the hot tub jets automatically shut off. Back to reality, I thought with a sigh.

"That was so relaxing," Rosalie told me as we grabbed our towels.

"Pure heaven," I said. "Let's do it again before we leave."

"Absolutely," she agreed.

As we toweled off, I was tempted to blurt out my secret. But a bunch of kids, all with freckles and red hair, burst into the room, and I lost my nerve. I'd wait until we reached Newport. Then Rosalie and I would have a long revealing walk on the beach.

Draping towels around our suits, we left Lucas playing with the freckled kids. Wet hair dribbled down my eyes as we hurried back to our room. I pulled my card key out, swiped the key in the electronic slot, opened the door—and saw Amber bending over a box. She jumped when she saw me and shoved the box behind her suitcase.

"What were you doing?" I asked, narrowing my gaze at my little sister.

"Nothing." Her violet blue eyes shifted toward her suitcase.

"Yeah, right. Amber, what's in the box?"

"Nothing."

Rosalie came up beside me and we shared a suspicious look.

"Nothing, huh?" I took a step closer to Amber's bed. "Then you won't mind if I look behind your—"

Before I could finish, Amber lunged sideways to block her suitcase. "Don't look! Go away!" she shouted.

"Why?" I demanded, straining my neck to look closer. "What are you hiding in there?"

She shook her head. "Nothing."

"What kind of a pet is it this time?" I persisted. "You better let it out of that box or it will suffocate."

"I don't got anything living. Honest."

"Double pinky swear on the life of all of your pets?"

She lifted both of her pinky fingers, crossed them, and nodded solemnly. She may be sneaky, but she wasn't a liar. She sounded so truthful, I had to believe her. Even Rosalie looked convinced.

Still, Amber wouldn't let us see the box, and I had a bad feeling.

Like trouble was just around the corner.

Waiting for me.

chapter four
# See Monsters

After a marathon of driving, we finally reached Newport later the next day.

"Where's the beach?" I asked, peering out my window as we turned onto a main road lined with businesses. The sky was gray, billowing with dark clouds and no hint of sunshine.

"Out there," Dad said, pointing past buildings. But all I could see was a haze of dreary gray. If the ocean was out there, it was hiding in the fog.

"What should we do now?" Dad asked with a glance at his wristwatch as he slowed for a stoplight.

"We could go on a lighthouse tour," Mom suggested.

"Let's save that for later," Dad said. "I know something else we can do. But it could be scary."

Lucas slapped down his *Peter Pan* script. "I love anything scary!"

"How scary?" I rubbed my hands together in delicious excitement.

"Very," Mom answered gravely.

"Maybe too scary." Dad turned to look at us with a solemn expression, but his eyes twinkled so I knew he was teasing.

"Nothing's too scary for us," I told him.

"Are you sure? Are you brave enough to face cannibals, rotting corpses, and sea monsters?"

"Ferocious crocodiles fear nothing," Lucas said, baring his teeth as he slipped into his reptile role.

"Bring on the monsters!" Rosalie exclaimed.

"Yeah! Cool!" I raised my hand and high-fived Rosalie. "The scarier the better."

"Well, that's three votes out of four." Mom turned toward my little sister whose violet eyes were wide as she hugged her stuffed bear. "What about you, Amber?"

The van hushed. Everyone turned to my little sister. I crossed my fingers and prayed that she wouldn't mess this up. Sometimes she had nerves of steel, but other times she'd burst into tears over something as silly as a sad song.

"Well, Amber?" Mom asked gently. "Do you want to go or would scary creatures frighten you?"

Amber shook her blond head.

"What does *that* mean?" I demanded with an impatient snort. "Yes or no?"

"Oh, yes." She flashed an eager grin. "Can I pet a sea monster?"

* * *

We drove south and made a right turn before a huge bridge, curving down to a wharf with a strong fish smell, sharp wind, and a damp cold that made me shiver as I stepped out of the van. The fog was lifting and beyond the buildings I glimpsed boats swaying on rough, gray-blue water. I looked around at cute shops selling food and souvenirs. Nothing the least bit scary.

"We're going that way," Dad told us, pointing up the narrow, business-lined street.

There were other tourists milling around, too. Some pushed baby strollers, held hands, or peered through store windows. We were like a small parade as we walked along the sidewalk, passing specialty shops with furniture, antiques, candy, and even one cute shop filled with cat items. Amber begged to go inside and look at "all the kitties," but my parents promised we'd shop later.

When I saw the sign announcing Undersea Gardens and Ripley's Museum, I was interested but also disappointed. I'd almost forgotten this was a business trip for Dad. "Oh, now I get it," I said with a sigh.

"Get what?" Rosalie asked, while my parents went to buy tickets.

"Dad is only taking us here because of his job. His show on famous fakes." I frowned, a bit embarrassed. Sometimes I wished I had a normal family like Rosalie. The Rippletoes had their own family softball team, volunteered for community events, and enjoyed backyard barbecues. They didn't go on trips in search of freaky paranormal happenings.

Ripley's Museum was freaky in a fun way. On the tour we saw shrunken heads, were jolted by a mock earthquake, played music on a magical harp, and shrieked when a rotting mummy jumped out at us.

Dad had a great time lecturing about ancient civilizations and peculiar burial rituals. If he hadn't been a TV host, I bet he would have been a history teacher. The stuff he said was interesting, but my mind wandered and I wondered when we'd see the mermaid. Dad had confided that was the main reason for our trip. "An authentic fake mermaid will make a great subject for my show," he'd explained.

*How could something be both authentic and fake?* I puzzled. And how could anyone fake a mermaid? You couldn't just fake a mermaid by slapping a fish tail on a girl and putting her in a swimming tank. Her skin would get all wrinkly after a while. And even really good swimmers had to come up for air every few minutes. No one would be fooled by someone wearing scuba gear.

I couldn't wait to see this "authentic fake." I imagined a beautiful mermaid with glowing hair flowing like golden rain over shimmery fish fins. She'd have luminous pearl skin, ruby-red lips, and sparkling sea-green eyes. And when she saw me, she would flash a lovely, mysterious smile, inviting me to be her friend and explore a glorious undersea world together.

But this blissful fantasy faded when I turned a corner and stopped abruptly in front of a rectangular case with a plaque that read The Fiji Mermaid.

She was smiling at me all right, but there was nothing lovely about her hideous, sharp, yellow teeth or her vicious, bony face.

She wasn't a *mermaid*.

She was a *mer-monster!*

## chapter five
# Fish Tales

"Ooh, creepy!" I exclaimed with disgust. This bunch of bones was nothing like the beautiful mermaid of my imagination. It was a withered fish skeleton about three feet long. Bony, ugly, and GROSS!

"What kind of fish is that?" Amber pointed at the glass case.

"It's supposed to be a mermaid," Dad explained. "But in actuality, it's a fish tail attached to a monkey body."

"Poor little monkey fish. That must have hurt," Amber said sadly.

"Not at all." Dad fondly patted her blond head. "The fish and monkey were long dead."

Lucas laughed. "Watch out, Dad or Amber will want to pet the furry fish."

I stared uneasily at the fake mermaid. Her expression creeped me out, as if she was plotting to sink her horrible teeth into my skin or slash her razor tail at me. She was nothing like the sweet mermaids I'd seen in cartoons. Instead, she oozed evil.

"How could anyone think it was real?" Lucas asked skeptically.

"Oh, they did." Dad chuckled. "P.T. Barnum could convince people of anything. He displayed this little gal in his museum and visitors flocked to see her. It's rumored that the original mermaid was larger than this and that there are at least seven Fiji mermaids. P.T. Barnum had a talent for entertaining people while he fooled them."

"Doesn't sound very honest," Mom said, her brows knitting together. "He reminds me of Sebastian Mooncraft."

"Not even close," Dad said firmly. He used to work with Mooncraft, but now they were sworn enemies with rival TV shows. "Mooncraft doesn't care about entertainment. *Mooncraft's Miracles* is just a scam to get rich by deceiving people."

"I doubt he's getting rich. His ratings aren't as high as yours," Mom said loyally.

"With shows on tap-dancing zombies and giant cannibal lizards, he doesn't deserve to be on TV." Dad's expression grew fierce. "He's a fraud. I only wish I could prove it."

Mom squeezed his arm. "You will, honey."

Hand in hand, my parents left the room. Lucas, Amber, and Rosalie trailed after them. But I paused to take one last look at the wicked-looking Fiji Mermaid. Her hollow, dark eyes seemed to warn: *I'm watching you—beware!*

With a shiver, I turned away and hurried to catch up with Rosalie.

It was a relief to step outside into hazy sunshine and crisp, salty air. We crossed the street and walked over a bridge to enter a ship that had been converted for the Undersea Show. The bright lights and tourist atmosphere made me feel normal again. We walked downstairs into the ship's hull. It was like a big aquarium, only the fish were in the ocean outside and we were dry and cozy inside. We could view swarming sea life through windows that circled the entire room.

Lights dimmed as we sat on a front bench to watch the show. A scuba diver splashed into a tank swarming with crabs, octopus, starfish, sturgeon, and more. Bubbles rose from his air tank as he told us about different sea creatures. He gestured to a wolf eel that looked vicious but was surprisingly gentle. Naturally, Amber wanted to pet it.

When the show ended, we filed back upstairs into a gift shop where we bought souvenirs. Amber chose a cuddly stuffed eel, Lucas wanted a wind-up shark, Rosalie bought a Frisbee, and I finally decided on a statue of a mermaid with long, golden hair and an angelic smile. No wicked teeth or razor-sharp tail.

Then we headed to our hotel.

Rosalie, Amber, and I had a room with a connecting door adjacent to the room my parents shared with Lucas. There were two queen-sized beds with striped blue bedspreads and painted seascapes on the walls. In the bathroom, we found little bottles of shampoo, crème rinse, and body lotion.

"Mom told me these are complimentary," I told Rosalie, gesturing to the bottles.

"Cool." Rosalie squirted apricot lotion on her hands. "I can't wait to hit the shops, too. When can we start on the three S's?"

*Four S's*, I thought to myself. *Swimming, shopping, sightseeing . . . and secrets.*

"As soon as Mom and Dad are ready," I told her as we walked over to our suitcases and started to unpack.

Rosalie and I were sharing the bed by the window. Amber had already decorated her side of the room with stuffed animals. Now she was doing her neat-freak thing—arranging tidy piles of shirts, pants, socks, and underwear in a drawer.

"I'm getting ready for the beach." Rosalie grabbed her swimsuit.

"The water is supposed to be freezing," I warned her.

"Who cares? By the time my brothers and sisters take baths, all the hot water is gone. I'm used to cold water."

I chuckled. "Okay, we'll swim until we turn into Popsicles. Then we can wade in the surf and look for seashells."

"Or play Frisbee." Rosalie spun her Frisbee into in the air, then gracefully caught it between two fingers.

I glanced out the window and noticed the fog had burned off and sunshine glittered off the ocean. I couldn't wait to go outside with Rosalie. I was so glad she'd come along on this trip. We were going to have so much fun.

Or so I thought for all of about five minutes . . . .

Then Mom peeked into the room and said she and Dad were leaving for business meetings. This didn't bother me—until she told us to stay at the hotel until they returned. No shopping, sightseeing, or splashing on the beach.

And I was stuck babysitting Amber.

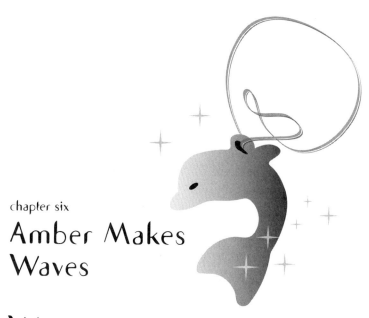

chapter six

# Amber Makes Waves

Why had I been cursed with a little sister?

My parents might have allowed Rosalie, Lucas, and I to go out alone (we were almost teenagers after all!). But Amber was too young and had to be watched. Amber didn't even seem to care that she was responsible for ruining my life. After our parents left, she grabbed a paper bag and ducked into the bathroom. If I hadn't been so upset, I would have wondered what was in the bag and why she had locked the door.

"My parents are SO unfair," I complained to Rosalie. "All they think about is work. I wish they were more like your parents."

"No, you don't," she said with a chuckle. "My parents make everything a competition. Like who can be the first to make their bed. Or they organize garbage races—whoever dumps the most garbage wins a prize."

"Sounds like fun."

"Unless you're the one who comes in last. Just for once, I'd like to come in first."

"Your brothers and sisters only win because they're older."

"I hate being the youngest. I'd rather be the oldest like you."

"No, you wouldn't. Then you'd get stuck babysitting." I shot an annoyed glance toward the bathroom where I heard water running. Amber could be flooding the bathroom for all I cared. I didn't want to be in charge of her anyway.

"Cheer up, Cassie," Rosalie said with a soft pat on my shoulder. "We can still have fun."

"Doing what?" I sulked, flopping across my bed. "I didn't come to the beach to spend all day inside."

"Your parents will only be gone a few hours. And they said we had to stay at the hotel, not in our rooms." Rosalie's dark eyes twinkled. "Let's go in the pool. It was great swimming at the last hotel."

"Yeah," I agreed. "And my parents won't mind as long as we all go together."

"I'll go get Lucas." Jumping up, Rosalie crossed over to the door connecting our two rooms. She gave the door a quick rap. When she explained to my brother what we wanted to do, he spit out his plastic crocodile teeth and tossed aside his script. Then he hurried to get his swim trunks.

*Okay, so maybe the day wasn't ruined,* I thought. Mom and Dad would be back in a few hours; then we'd go down to the beach. In the meantime, hanging out in a heated pool would be fun.

I wore my green-striped suit I'd been given last April when I turned eleven, and Rosalie's silver bikini looked great against her golden-brown skin.

Since this might be a good time to reveal my secrets to Rosalie, I tucked the crystal ball in my jacket pocket.

Rosalie tossed her beach towel over her shoulders and I wore my jacket over my suit like a cover-up. We started to leave, until I realized we'd forgotten something.

Or *someone* to be exact.

I whirled around and rapped on the bathroom door. "Amber, get out of there!"

"Go away," came her muffled reply.

"We're gonna swim. Come out and get your suit on."

She didn't answer and I heard rustling paper and the soft swish of water. What was she doing in there anyway?

I smacked my fist on the door. "Amber, if you don't come out right now, I'm going to get a key from the office and drag you out!"

"No!" she exclaimed.

"Open the door."

"Go away and leave me alone."

"Forget it! I'm in charge of you, so you're going to come out right now. Then you're going to put on your suit and have fun swimming with us—whether you like it or not."

"Oh . . . all right." I heard odd bumps and a sharp bang. "In a few minutes."

I turned to Rosalie with a pained expression. "This could take a while. Go ahead to the pool with Lucas."

"I'll stay with you."

"Really, it's okay." I could tell she was impatient to leave by the way she kept shifting her feet. "No reason for both of us to wait around."

"Okay. See you soon!" Rosalie bolted for the door and I heard her greeting Lucas. Then the front door slammed shut with a bang. They were gone.

I folded my arms and tapped my foot as I waited for Amber to come out of the bathroom. I wasn't worried about her because she sounded okay and was too much of a neat freak to make a mess. But she was acting weirder than usual.

Then the bathroom door opened. Amber flashed a sweet smile, the image of innocence—which proved she was up to something sneaky.

I studied her closely, on the alert for anything odd. But there were no telltale feathers (like when she'd smuggled our duck on a campout) and there were no weird marks on her skin or missing chunks of her hair (like when she hid the alien pet). Still, I remembered her secret meeting with Olivia and their puzzling trade. Some freaky pet that had three eyes. But where was it now?

"What were you doing for so long?" I asked suspiciously.

"Washing my hands."

"Where's the paper bag you took in with you?"

"What bag?" She widened her blue eyes. "I don't know what you're talking about."

"Oh, yes you do!" I strode into the bathroom. The room was clean and tidy; nothing looked out of place. I looked in the trash can and under the sink. No bag.

My gaze zeroed in on the tub. The plastic shower curtain had been open earlier, but now it was closed. Definitely suspicious.

When I moved toward the bathtub, Amber jumped in my way.

I pushed her aside and reached for the shower curtain.

Then I yanked it open.

chapter seven
# Water Babies

All I saw was a glass bowl of water and a crumpled brown bag.

"Why are you hiding a water bowl? Where's your pet?" I put my hands on my hips as I faced my little sister. "And don't tell me you don't have one because I overheard you talking to Olivia. I know you traded with her. Although I can't figure out how you smuggled a pet without me finding it."

"I hid it inside a puzzle box." Amber's lower lip quivered and she looked close to tears.

"But that's cruel! How could any pet breathe in a box?"

"It . . . It wasn't alive."

"You brought a DEAD pet on our vacation!"

"Not dead, just not born. I had to mix it with water." She pointed to the glass bowl. "I'm growing babies."

"Baby what?" Sighing, I raked my fingers through my hair. "I don't understand. There's nothing in that water."

"Not yet. It has to sit for 24 hours."

"You are so *not* making any sense. You can't grow babies in water."

"Yeah, I can." She nodded, then pulled out a small printed paper from her pocket. "See! This came with the kit."

"A kit?" Puzzled, I took the paper and read:

*Amazing Living Sea Monkeys! Just add water and watch them grow!*

"Sea monkeys?" I murmured, beginning to understand. I'd seen an advertisement once for these weird pets, but thought it was all a trick. I didn't believe living creatures could be created from a kit.

"I'm a momma!" Amber said with a proud look at the glass bowl. "Tomorrow I'll have babies."

"Are you sure this will work?" I asked doubtfully, glancing at the directions that included a 24-hour wait, adding a special pouch, stirring, then letting them sit in sunlight.

"Olivia's done it lots and told me everything. My monkey babies will be pretty."

"Pretty weird, you mean."

"I'll be a good momma and clean their water and love them. They'll get so big they'll grow three eyes. I'm going to name them after my favorite TV show—Velma, Shaggy, and Scooby. Just don't tell Mom and Dad," she added with a protective glance at the glass bowl. "Okay?"

"Well . . ." I paused to think. This was a golden opportunity. I didn't care whether Amber had sea monkeys or not. But I did care about her causing problems that might ruin our vacation.

So I made her a deal. My secrecy in exchange for her obedience. She had to be on her best behavior for the rest of this trip. If I asked her to do something, she had to do it. No arguments.

And amazingly, she agreed.

\* \* \*

When Amber and I finally made it to the indoor hotel pool, Lucas was hanging out with some boys his age and Rosalie was swimming with a dark-skinned girl with short, spiky black hair and shiny almond-brown eyes. The girl looked older, like an eighth grader.

I told Amber to play in the shallow water, and instead of arguing like she would have done before our agreement, she obediently doggie paddled off. Then I jumped in the deep end and swam over to Rosalie.

"Cassie, meet Georgia." Rosalie gestured excitedly.

"Hey, Cassie!" Georgia said in a squeaky voice that sounded like Minnie Mouse crossed with a cheerleader. When she waved at me, she splashed my face. Water swooshed up my nose and I tasted chlorine.

"Sorry about that." Georgia's laugh didn't sound very sorry at all. "Are you okay?"

"Yeah." I nodded, wiping my stinging eyes.

"Wait till you hear, Cassie." Rosalie held onto the rim of the pool and kicked her feet in small flutters. "Georgia is into sports and plays on a volleyball team. That's why she's here—her team is stopping for a few days on their way back from a big competition. And they won first place!"

"Great," I said without any enthusiasm as I waded in place.

"So Cass," Georgia said. "What sport do you play?"

I shrugged. "I like swimming and riding my bike."

"Cycling is ultra cool! I went on a 50K over spring break. But I prefer team sports and everyone says I'm the best server on our team. You play volleyball?"

"Volleyball? Oh . . . a few times. I played it in school."

"Cassie isn't really into sports," Rosalie said, playfully splashing at me. "She says I'm like obsessed."

"Me, too!" Georgia said. "So that makes us like twin jocks."

Then they launched into talk about some famous volleyball players, who couldn't be that famous because I'd never heard of them. I ducked underwater and swam around. When I popped back up, they were still talking sports. It was like they were speaking a foreign language.

So I swam a few laps. When I joined them again, they were laughing like crazy. I pushed dripping hair from my eyes and asked, "What's so funny?"

"It's a long story," Rosalie said between giggles.

"You wouldn't understand," Georgia added.

I did not like the way Georgia was grinning at *my* best friend. Couldn't she get her own best friend? What about her teammates? They had to be around the hotel somewhere—unless she bored them to death with all her jockette jargon.

Still, we would only be here for a short time so I could be generous and share my best friend. When my parents returned, we'd all go on a tour of a haunted lighthouse. That would be really fun—especially without Georgia.

So I swam over to Amber and we played "Dive for Pennies" until Dad showed up. With the same dramatic tone he used to make startling announcements on his TV show, he told us that business was over for the day. "It's time for family fun. So get out of the pool."

"Sure!" I said eagerly, jumping out of the water and toweling off.

Lucas waved to his swim pals and Rosalie told Georgia good-bye.

"Remember what I said," Georgia called out.

"I won't forget," she promised.

"Forget what?" I asked as I handed Rosalie her towel.

Before she could answer, Amber ran over whining that she couldn't find her towel. Naturally, babysitting-slave Cassie had to help her look. Only it wasn't by the chair where she swore she left it. Lucas and Rosalie went ahead with Dad while I searched under every chair. But the towel wasn't anywhere. I was ready to scream in frustration when I looked over and saw Amber laughing.

"What's so funny?" I snarled.

"I just remembered—I didn't bring a towel!"

Glaring, I tossed my towel at her.

When we hurried down the carpeted hall toward our rooms, I heard voices coming from my mom and dad's room and noticed that their door was propped open. Peaking inside, I saw Rosalie deep in a conversation with my parents. The excited way they were all smiling made me uneasy.

"What's going on?" I asked, stepping inside with Amber.

"Rosalie just told us her wonderful news," Mom said, her smile widening.

"What news?" I asked.

Mom raised her brows. "Didn't Rosalie tell you?"

"No. She did *not*," I said with a sharp look at Rosalie.

"Sorry. I didn't have a chance." Rosalie's smile faded. "Everything happened so fast. I only just found out Ariel had a sprained ankle and the Carter twins were sick."

"Ariel who?" I blinked in bewilderment. "What twins?"

"Georgia's teammates," she answered as if that all made sense.

Mom nodded. "And your father and I agree it's a wonderful opportunity for Rosalie. So instead of going on a lighthouse tour, we'll watch the tournament."

"Tournament?" I asked warily.

"Yes." Mom reached out to hug Rosalie. "There's a beach volleyball tournament at three o'clock. And Rosalie's been invited to play."

chapter eight
# Galena

Everyone was excited about the volleyball tournament.

Except me.

I knew it was selfish to want Rosalie all to myself. And I wished I could be happy for her. But I
kept remembering how she and Georgia joked about
having so much in common they were like twins.
Their laughter totally shut me out. Was I losing my
best friend?

*Not if I can help it!* I thought as I slipped through the connecting door to my room and sank onto my bed. *I'll show Rosalie I can be a jock, too. I'll get into shape and join her teams so we can do everything together. I can lift weights to bulk up and watch the sports channel instead of the travel channel.*

Rosalie and I used to be together so much, people confused our names, calling me Rosalie and her Cassie. But things started to change this summer. While I was on a family campout, Rosalie joined Club Glorious and made new friends. I'd wanted to join, too, but my parents didn't approve of an exclusive health club. I got tired of feeling left out, so I came up with the idea to bring the "Glorious Girls" to my house. I had a treasure hunting party and we all had a great time. After that my friendship with Rosalie grew stronger than ever—until Georgia showed up.

And the last thing I wanted to do was watch a dumb volleyball game.

So while everyone else arranged beach towels on the sand and prepared to watch the game, I slipped away.

The sun shone warm, but a chilly wind slapped my skin and I was glad I'd brought my jacket. When I tucked my hands into the pockets, I touched a smooth round object. I reached inside and pulled out the crystal globe. I'd forgotten it was in my pocket. I'd planned to show it to Rosalie when I told her my secrets. But if she'd rather be with Georgia, that was her loss. I wouldn't tell her anything.

Resentment mounted. I kicked sand and walked away from the excited shouts from the volleyball game. Watching a dumb game had *not* been part of my plans. I'd had such high hopes for this vacation—all including Rosalie. But she'd made her choice, and it wasn't me.

The more I thought about Rosalie and Georgia, the faster I walked. The ocean roared in my head and foamy waves crashed against jagged rocks. Seagulls circled high and screeched like they were in a bad mood. I left the sandy beach; the shoreline grew rocky and narrow. I carefully skip-hopped across salt-sprayed black rocks and pressed close to a sharp cliff to keep dry.

When I stopped and looked back, the crowded beach had vanished. I was alone on a rocky stretch of sand. All I could see was wet black rocks and wild, foamy waves. I kept on, passing tide pools with tiny scurrying crabs and jagged mossy boulders. Balancing carefully, I climbed or jumped over steep boulders. Icy wind shivered through my jacket and my fingers ached from the cold. When I tucked my hands into my pockets, I felt the crystal ball. And it was *warm!*

When I lifted it and peered inside, a golden light flickered from its silvery depths. The globe had been cloudy and lifeless since leaving the magical community inside Mount Shasta. But now the globe glimmered with magic. My heart thumped as I watched for visions to appear.

"What are you looking at?"

"Who said that?" Startled, I shoved the crystal globe back in my pocket and whirled around. But no one was there. I turn the other direction and still didn't see anybody.

"Yoo hoo! Down here," the voice called again.

Then I saw her. Far below the cliff I stood on, surrounded by a half circle of craggy rocks, a girl swam in the deep gray-green ocean. She had long violet-blue hair, a face that shone like a pale moon, and full peach lips curved in a smile. She waved at me, her fingertips glittering with purple nail polish.

"Oh, sorry," I said awkwardly. "I didn't know anyone else was here."

"I just popped up." She chuckled and I thought how nice her voice sounded. Not an annoying chirp like Georgia's, but as soothing as wind chimes. I couldn't stop staring at her. Even with wet hair and no makeup, she was stunningly beautiful, like a movie star or runway model.

I knelt down over the rocky ledge, noticing her odd swimming suit top strung together with rope and seashells. "Aren't you cold?" I asked.

"Never." She shook her violet-blue head. "The water feels great."

"Really? Dad told me it would be too cold for swimming without a wetsuit."

"I'm used to it." She grinned. "What's your name anyway?"

"Cassie."

"I'm Galena. Where are you from?"

"California."

"Ooh!" she squealed. "Where everyone is rich, wears fancy clothes, and lives in fabulous mansions?"

I laughed. "Maybe in Hollywood, but not in the northern part of the state where I live. No one I know is rich or has a mansion. Where are you from?"

She lifted her hands and gestured wide. "Around here."

"Cool! You're so lucky to live by the ocean. Do you swim every day?"

"I can't keep away," she said in a bored tone. "But it's lonely swimming by myself. Come join me."

The gray-green ocean churned with foamy waves, making it impossible to see beyond the dark, deep surface. Suddenly uneasy, I shook my head. "I'd rather not."

"Why? Are you afraid of the water?" Her long hair swirled around her like blue seaweed.

"No. I'm just not in the mood."

"You do seem kind of down." She gave me a long look. "Is something wrong."

"It's nothing important."

"Trouble with a friend?" she guessed.

I raised my brows. "How did you know?"

"I'm a good judge of human nature. Is it your best friend?"

"Yeah," I sighed, "At least I hope she's my best friend. I'm not sure anymore."

"I know what it's like." Galena's voice softened with sympathy. "I used to have a best friend."

"What happened?"

"Stelleri and I are cousins and we've played together since we were as small as tadpoles. But then she found new friends and turned against me. She spread ugly rumors about me."

"That's terrible!" I shuddered, unable to imagine Rosalie ever treating me that badly. But I never thought she'd ditch me on our vacation either.

"It's been awful and now I'm all alone with no friends."

"That's not true." Impulsively, I reached out my hand toward Galena. "I'll be your friend."

"Really?" A beautiful smile lit up her face. "Great!"

With a joyful whoop, she splashed and then dove underwater. Her violet-blue hair trailed like a silky veil behind her as she curled in a somersault. She moved so fast I couldn't see her feet. But I did see something else—a huge, gray fish tail. Like a shark! A giant fish whisked through the waves behind her.

"Galena! It's chasing you! Watch out!"

"For what?" she asked, popping back up.

"That fish! I saw a huge tail . . . there is it again!" I pointed at the silver-green fin that glittered behind her.

But she didn't cry out in fear or even swim away. Instead, she laughed. Then she leaned backwards and up popped the giant fish tail. Only there wasn't any fish! The tail was attached to Galena!

I gasped.

She was a mermaid!

## chapter nine

# Beware of
# False Gifts

"**Y**ou don't have legs . . . you have fins!" I gasped.

"Of course," she said with a shrug.

"But . . . But you can't be a mermaid!"

"Why can't I?" she asked with an indignant huff.

"Because mermaids aren't real."

"Do I look plastic?"

"No . . . but it's impossible!" My eyes stung with salty spray and shock.

"Carp crud!" She slapped her tail against the sea. "I don't know why you even have eyes in your head, because you clearly see nothing. You land people assume you are so special that nothing else exists."

"I know other things exist, but I never expected . . . I mean . . ." I stared at her shimmery tail. "You really are a mermaid?"

"Well, duh." She flipped her silky violet-blue hair over her shoulder. "Only I prefer the term 'mer-person.' I am not *anyone's* maid."

"I'm sorry, I didn't mean . . . this is all so strange."

"Do I scare you? Are you going to freak out and run away?"

"No." I shook my head, amazed and honored to meet such a fantastical girl. I wished I could show her to Dad. He would be blown away! He'd have to change his TV show title to *I* Do *Believe It!*

Questions bubbled up inside of me. What was it like to live in the ocean? Were other mermaids beautiful like Galena? Did they spend all day having fun or did they have to go to school? Did mermaids have homework?

But all I could do was stare with my mouth half open.

Galena arched her silvery brows, regarding me cautiously. "So are we still friends?"

"Well . . . yeah, if you don't mind hanging out with a land dweller. I could really use a friend right now."

"So could I. And I would never ditch you."

"Rosalie probably doesn't even know I'm gone." I sighed, scooting down on the edge of a rock so my legs dangled near Galena. "She's totally obsessed with sports. Because of her oh-so-important game, we can't go on a lighthouse tour. I really, really wanted to go there today."

"I've swam near lighthouses and visitors always seem to be having fun."

"I'll bet they are. But the museum will be closed by the time Rosalie's game is over. Then it'll be dark and we'll have to go back to the hotel."

"Rosalie sounds very selfish, only thinking about herself. How tragically unfair."

"That's for sure."

"She should think of your feelings."

"You're right." My anger crashed like the waves slamming against the rocks. "I invited her on my vacation so we could do stuff together and now she's doing stuff with other people. She's ruining everything."

"She does not deserve you. If you were my best friend, I would never disappoint you and we would do amazing things you can't even imagine."

"Like what?" I asked curiously.

"I'd show you how to breathe underwater and ride dolphins."

"Wow! That would be so cool!"

"I know that 'cool' means superior from listening to surface dwellers. I am fascinated by your customs and language."

"Superior," I said, grinning.

"For a long time, I've dreamed of meeting someone like you." Galena gazed up at me with a dreamy expression. "Sometimes, I swim near boats and watch through the windows. I can see the picture box you call a TV. There is so much life beyond the sea, worlds with tall buildings and airplanes and shopping malls. It's all so glamorous."

"Glamorous? You're gotta be joking."

"It's not funny to have fins instead of feet." She flipped up her tail and pointed to her fins. "I dream of wearing high heels, sneakers, boots, slippers, and sandals. You are so lucky to have feet."

"Lucky?" I glanced down at my water-soaked flip-flops and saw that my toes were crusted with sand. "Shoes are no big deal. But riding a dolphin would be the most thrilling thing in the universe."

"Perhaps to you," she said with a mysterious smile as she scooted up on a rock. "But not if you were in my shoes . . . or fins."

I shook my head, imagining the freedom of gliding in the ocean on the back of a dolphin. I'd heard in a science class that the world was 80 percent water—which meant I was only living a 20 percent life.

Galena was sighing. "I envy the beautiful beach people," she confided. "I watch them have picnics and dance to music players. They wear such lovely clothes, jewelry, and hair baubles."

I thought of Bobble Head Dolls. "Baubles?" I questioned.

"Fancy decorative objects." She pointed. "Like the pink ornament in your hair."

"My scrunchie?" I reached up to touch the cloth band. "It's nothing special."

"It dazzles with the colors of a rainbow fish and holds your hair so snug. My hair tangles and snags on coral."

"I now what you need." I loosened my scrunchie and held it out to her. "Here."

"You are gifting me?" she asked in hushed awe.

"Sure. It'll stop your hair from getting tangled."

"It's so beautiful!" She looked so excited as she took the scrunchie, you'd think I'd given her a winning lottery ticket. "No one has ever been so kind to me. I must reward you."

"You don't have to," I said quickly. "It's only worth like a dollar."

"You're a real friend, Cassie, and you deserve something special for your thoughtfulness. I know!" She held out her arm and lifted off a slim bracelet shaped like a dolphin. It shone silver and sparkled with tiny twin diamonds in the dolphin's eyes.

"That's so beautiful," I murmured in awe.

"I am honored to gift you."

"Oh, I couldn't take it. It must be valuable."

"A friend is worth far more," she said sincerely. "Here. Put it on."

"I don't know . . ." Temptation softened my tone. The jewels danced with sparkling light and the silver dolphin seemed to wink at me. Rosalie would be so envious when she saw me wearing such a pretty bracelet, especially when she found out it came from a mermaid.

Still, it felt wrong to accept such an expensive gift, so I shook my head. "Sorry. I just can't . . ."

"But you must!" Galena insisted with startling fierceness.

Her violet eyes blazed like bonfires as she leapt up, balancing like a gymnast on her shimmery tail, and shoved the bracelet on my wrist. She raised her arms toward the sky and chanted in a high, breathy voice:

*Mystic spirits of the deep,*
*bound forever secrets keep.*
*Burning fire under sea,*
*summon magick destiny.*

*Stormy tides of moon and night,*
*Bid my call, let dark ignite.*
*Powers old, from depths that dwell,*
*let souls exchange—cast sea switch spell.*

Dazzling sparks sizzled around the bracelet and dizziness cascaded in blinding waves. Galena's pale face loomed large, her smile twisting into a triumphant grin.

"What's . . . what's happening?" I called out as my world spun out of control and the ground beneath me quaked. I grabbed wildly for something to hold onto, only I was slipping, sliding off the rocks, splashing, sinking into the deep sea . . .

chapter ten
# Sea Change

Kicking, splashing, struggling, I fought an unknown enemy.

Was I drowning? Would Galena run for help? But how could she run when she had no legs? She'd have to swim. Darkness strangled me and I gagged on seawater. Panicked, I thrashed desperately. Everything was confusing. I spun in a cyclone, trapped and spiraling out of control. I couldn't see or think or feel anything except fear.

Sinking deep, deep down into nothing—I had to reach the surface. Only which way was up? I was lost in a void of green sea. My heart hammered and terror ripped through me. Were these my last minutes?

Bright light glared over head. I thought I'd died and was floating up to heaven until I broke through waves. Gasping, I sucked in air. Wonderful, fresh air! And the light came from the sun shining. Sputtering, I struggled to swim for shore, only it was beyond sight. Where was land? Had I drifted miles out to sea in only a few minutes?

"Gal . . . Galena! Help!" I managed to shout before sea splashed into my mouth again and I felt myself slipping under. A wave crashed into me and I was blinded by salty water. I tried to kick, but my legs wouldn't work as if they'd turned to ice.

I thought I heard someone call my name and I fought to move toward the sound. Waves calmed and I saw a dark shape ahead. Was it the shore? I hoped so! But it seemed so far away. Could I get there before waves knocked me under again?

I swam on, growing weaker and weaker. My arms were heavy anchors dragging me down and I couldn't make my numb legs work. I felt so strange and weak . . .

*Keep going, don't give up,* I told myself. *It can't get any worse.*

But when I glanced over my shoulders, I saw movement and dark fins. A shark! It sliced through waves right behind me—a snack-sized bite away!

Energy surged and I paddled frantically. Sensing the predator closing in, I pushed myself faster. FASTER! My legs still felt numb, but fear propelled me to a super-warp-terror speed. Rocks jutted out like black shadows and foamy waves crested around me. I only slowed when a glance behind revealed empty sea.

The shark—or whatever it had been—was gone.

But when I looked around for Galena, I didn't see her either.

"Galena!" I hollered, treading water frantically in circles. Where was she? Why hadn't she tried to help me? Maybe she'd gotten scared and swam away. Or had something terrible happened to her?

I heard a shout and saw someone on the shore. A dark-haired girl who waved at me and looked strangely familiar. As I swam close enough to see her face, I gasped. She looked like me! Same wide smile and skinny legs. She even wore a green-striped suit exactly like mine.

But the biggest shock came when I looked down at myself and saw a stranger's pale skin, a skimpy top of seashells, and a glistening fish tail. No wonder my legs felt numb—they were gone. Instead I had fins!

I wasn't a girl anymore—I was a mermaid!

And Galena was *me*.

## chapter eleven
# Gimme Back My Body!

I expected Galena to freak out, too, but she grinned like someone told a funny joke. (Was I the punchline?)

"Do something!" I shouted, treading water desperately.

"I already did. I'm quite happy with your body." She bent down and gently touched her legs. "These feel a bit wobbly, but I am a fast learner and I will have plenty of time to practice walking."

"What's going on?" A wave slapped my face and I gagged on seawater. Grabbing a rock so I wouldn't sink, I demanded, "Galena, why do you look like me and I look like you?"

"I did it! The results are superior," she said proudly. "I've been waiting for a human like you to come along."

"But you . . . you said we were friends!"

"So I lied." She shrugged off the jacket I'd been wearing only moments ago and kicked it aside. "You are quite gullible. Moping around about silly friendships, when you had something I've longed for my whole life."

"What could you possibly want from me?" I stung from betrayal.

"Your legs." She gestured down, her lips twisting into a smug smile. "Well, actually MY legs now. Not much to look at, but oh-so-useful for getting around on land. With these I can go anywhere and have everything I desire."

"That poem you chanted! It was a magic spell!" I accused, tugging on the silver bracelet which stuck to my skin like extra-powerful Super Glue. "You tricked me!"

"It was far too easy. Didn't your parents ever warn you about talking to strangers?" She laughed in a harsh way that made her voice (my voice!) sound like a witch's cackle. That's what she was—a wicked witch! And she had *my* body!

"Give me back myself!" I pushed higher on the rock, then lost my grip and I slipped back into the sea.

"Not a chance! You accepted the trade when you took my gift. A gift in exchange for a gift. But since I'm so nice, you can have this back." She unwrapped the pink scrunchie from her (my!) hair and shot it back at me like a rubber band. "You'll need it more than I will."

"Watch out!" I dodged when the scrunchie almost hit my eye.

"Sorry," Galena said with a laugh that showed she wasn't sorry at all. "You should put that in your hair so it doesn't tangle. Mermaid hair is beautiful, but it can't be cut and is impossible to tame. Now I really have to go and get some fancy clothes and pretty baubles."

"No! You can't leave me like THIS!"

"Watch me." She laughed and turned away. I shouted, begged and pleaded, but she kept walking until she was out of sight.

Then I was alone—with a floppy tail instead of feet.

My heart sank and my eyes blurred with tears. How could Galena play such a horrible trick on me? She said she was my friend—and I'd believed her! She was right; I was gullible.

*Now what?* I thought as I clung to a rock. Where could I go? My own family wouldn't recognize me. I didn't even recognize myself! And I had no idea how to swim with a tail. It flopped and sagged awkwardly. If I released my hold on the rock, would I sink down to the bottom of the sea?

*Either way I'm sunk,* I thought miserably. *I can't stay here, yet I don't know how to leave. Galena will never trade back and my family will think she's me. They'll leave Newport and I'll still be stuck here.*

I would have clung to the rock forever if I hadn't noticed a bright flash on the beach. A small object glittered in the sand near my jacket.

"My crystal globe!" I murmured with renewed hope. It must have fallen from the pocket when Galena had tossed off my jacket.

The crystal had felt warm and sparkled earlier. Was the magic returning? The globe had the power to show visions of my deepest desire. But maybe it had other powers, too. Could it switch me back into my real body? This wild idea gave me the courage to release my death grip on the rock and swim for shore. Amazingly, I didn't sink.

Grabbing the globe, I peered inside . . . but saw nothing. No warmth or magical glow. A total dud. Whatever power had caused it to spark before was gone. And so were all my hopes.

Fighting not to cry, I bit my lip. Wallowing in self-pity wouldn't solve anything. The only way to get my body back was to find Galena. Only that was impossible . . . or was it?

I couldn't run without any legs, but I could swim.

Tucking the tiny crystal globe inside my seashell top, I tried to swim. It was awkward at first because my brain kept ordering my body to kick with two feet. I foundered on fins and swallowed seawater. I flopped over in a back float, only lost my balance and flipped over. More swallowed seawater.

Maybe I was going about this all wrong. I had to think like a mermaid—not a human—to swim with fins. So I shut off my brain and Galena's fins did their thing. Just like that—I was slicing through waves with the speed and grace of a dolphin.

Being a mermaid would have been cool, except that I was scared to death. As I cornered a towering cluster of rocks, a little boy tossing a ball to his dog on the beach pointed at me. He hollered for his mommy and his dog started barking.

I kept on swimming. A voice in my head warned me to stay out of sight, but there was no time for caution. If I didn't switch with Galena soon, she could go anywhere in the world and I could end up trapped in her body. Forever! I had to find her . . . FAST!

Desperately, I swam along the shoreline, searching for brown hair and a green swimsuit. But there was no sign of me. As I neared the more populated stretch of beach, I heard shouts from the volleyball game. My heart ached as I thought of my family and Rosalie. They were out there somewhere and had no idea I was in trouble. It reminded me of the time my sister was kidnapped by an alien. I was the only one who knew she was missing, and I'd eventually rescued her.

Would anyone rescue me?

Not if Galena reached my family first.

Swimming faster near the shore, I scanned the beach. I didn't see anyone familiar, but people began to notice me.

"A dolphin!" I heard a shout.

Someone else screamed. "Shark!"

"No, that's not a shark! It's a mermaid!"

A group gathered at the edge of the beach, gaping with astonishment. I quickly realized a new danger. There was a good reason why mermaids hid in the ocean. Humans wouldn't allow mermaids to live peacefully. No—people wanted to capture them and put them in aquariums.

*I'm not waiting around for a net!* I thought, turning away from the shore.

But two muscular guys in black wetsuits grabbed their surfboards and dove off after me. "Hey, I'm a normal girl!" I wanted to shout. But my big fish tail was kind of hard to hide. No one would believe I'd been magically transformed from a girl to half-fish.

So I sped up and tried to swim away. Only the surfboards sliced through the waves at amazing speeds. They were closing in! When I looked back to see where they were, one of the guys was so close I could see the pimples on his nose. He came closer, closer—merely a foot away. He balanced on his board and reached out . . .

Before he could touch me, a dark shape erupted from the sea with the force of a tidal wave. The surfer cried out as his board was swept aside. He toppled and splashed into the sea.

There was a quicksilver flash of white teeth and glinting gray eyes.

Then a hand shot up from the ocean and grabbed me.

chapter twelve

# Mer-Magic

I was being pulled down, down beneath the sea by something supernatural. We zoomed so rapidly I couldn't see my captor. Blurs of fish, coral, and wavering weeds swam at a dizzying pace. There was no time for anything except terror. When we slowed, and my mind caught up with reality, I could finally see the figure beside me. Not a monster as I feared, but a merman. Or actually a mer-boy since he didn't look much older than me.

"Who? What's happening?" My words blew bubbles that sounded almost as clear as speaking above water.

"A simple thank you would be nice for a change."

"Why should I thank you for trying to drown me?" I shook my head, confused to discover I hadn't drowned and was in fact breathing underwater. "Who are you?"

"I find no humor in your games, Galena."

"I'm not Galena!"

"Nice try." He gave a skeptical laugh. He was kind of cute, with wavy green-blue hair, shiny gray eyes, and dimples. He wore no shirt and smooth muscles rippled in his arms and firm stomach. Not the time to notice a cute guy, but I was only human (sort of).

"I'm not a mermaid."

"I know—a mer-person," he said with a wink. "You're nobody's maid."

"That's not what I meant. I'm not a real mermaid."

"So you're a fake?" He chuckled. "You don't need to pretend with me, Lena. I'll stick by you no matter what."

"But I'm not her!" I insisted, pushing back strands of violet-blue hair that floated in my eyes. "I'm human! You have to help me."

"Helping you is my worst habit." He wagged a finger at me. "What were you thinking up there? Those humans almost captured you! You're already in enough trouble without risking such a serious violation. You know better."

"No I don't, because I'm NOT Galena!" I was too angry to stop to marvel at the fact I was arguing with a mer-guy. If I ever got out of this mess, I would be amazed by the whole experience. But now I just wanted my life—and my body—back.

"Why do you make everything so difficult?" he asked, floating sideways and plucking a wavy green sprout of seaweed. He plopped it in his mouth like a stick of licorice. He reached out toward me. "Come on. I'll take you home."

*Home?* I puzzled. What exactly was home for a mermaid? Did mer-people have houses with back-yards and bedrooms? Or was it like the legends of Atlantis with elegant temples, spiral columns, and marble mansions?

Despite my fears, curiosity stirred. There was no going back to my life as long as I looked like Galena, so I might as well go forward with the mer-guy. Maybe he could help me reverse the magic and restore my body.

"What's your name?" I asked as we swam down so deep the sea dimmed from day to twilight. Although I could barely see him, I clung to his hand like a lifeline.

"As if you didn't know," he said sharply.

"Maybe I have amnesia and can't remember anything about you."

"Oh, all right, I'll play along. I'm Astor."

"You probably won't believe me, but my real name is Cassie."

"Right. I don't believe you,"

A school of glowing fish whizzed by, tickling my fins. I almost smiled at the wonder of this hidden world, but I was still scared. Instead of blue sky overhead, I was surrounded by gray-green sea. Seaweed waved in underwater currents and there were dizzying flashes of silver, yellow, and red fish. How long would I have to stay here? Would I ever get my own body back?

"So how much farther?" I asked.

"Not far enough for you," he said ominously.

Alarm jabbed me like a sharp fishhook. "What's that supposed to mean?"

Astor shook his head, then turned away. For a long time we swam in silence. The deeper we swam, the darker the water. I couldn't see anything, not even myself. I was sinking fast into an eerie world that both terrified and thrilled me. I was actually going to see a secret community of mer-people! I had no idea what to expect, except that it would be amazing. And hopefully someone would know how to reverse Galena's spell.

Pushing fear aside, I pretended to be brave.

Up ahead, a light bobbed, glowing bigger and brighter as we drew near. Darkness lifted and I glimpsed a school of tiny yellow and black fish dart through craggy coral. Smooth rocks and pale sand shone on the sea floor like polished tile, and there was a soft sound of humming—like a choir singing.

"What's that noise?" I asked.

"You know." Astor spit out a clump of green seaweed.

"Maybe I want to hear you explain it to me."

"Galena, is this another trick?"

"No trick, I guess I'm just forgetful. Everything is new to me—being underwater, talking to you, and that humming sound. Where is it coming from?"

"Our light source," he said simply. "No one will believe you have amnesia. You often complain that my enjoyment of facts bores you, so be warned. If you keep asking questions, I may answer them."

"Please, do. Tell me about the light."

"Very well." His pale brows arched with puzzlement as we continued to swim together. "You asked for it. We learned all about it in basic science, how hundreds of years ago our world used to be bright with light from the sun and the moon. But the waters gradually grew dark from misuse from surface dwellers."

"How?" I asked.

"They darkened the waters by spilling oil, trash, and sewage into the ocean. Our civilization might have died except for wise scientists who discovered a way of harnessing underground natural gases into a deep canyon. They called this energy Heartlight. Many lives were lost and decades passed before connecting tubes of Heartlight were completed. Now it brightens our days and powers our tools. Without it, our community would have perished long ago. Are you bored yet?"

"No. It's amazing! I want to hear more."

"You're acting very strange."

"That's because I am Strange . . . Cassie Strange."

He sighed. I gave up trying to convince him and stared at this incredible world. Towering rock formations like high-rise buildings circled in a fortress around a glowing canyon, as if the moon had crashed down from the sky into the sea floor. *Heartlight,* I guessed.

There were no houses or buildings. The mer-people blended in with their environment, creating dwellings in the towering rocky hills that jutted as tall as skyscrapers. I glimpsed lit round windows and imagined mer-people gliding from room to room, cozy in their underwater paradise.

I heard an odd sound and looked up to see three amazing beings swimming toward us. "Wow!" I exclaimed in awe. "Three more mer-people!"

"Oh, oh," Astor murmured. "A trio of trouble."

But I ignored him and turned to marvel at the merman and two mermaids. The mermaids wore shell tops like mine and the merman was shirtless with flabby pale skin. His long, green-gray beard swayed to his knees like a fuzzy ribbon. The largest mermaid reminded me of a manatee—tuffs of silver hair framing a chubby face with two chins and black, black eyes. The smaller mermaid was very plain with protruding buckteeth. She seemed young, timid, and fragile.

The trio had one thing in common: hostile glares aimed at me.

I gulped nervously, remembering Astor's comment about trouble waiting for Galena. Was this "unwelcome committee" what he meant? I turned to ask, only he was disappearing around a clump of sea flowers. Swimming away instead of standing by me.

Coward! I wanted to yell.

The fact that he was afraid magnified my own fears. I better get out of here!

"Galena, halt!" ordered the bearded merman.

Trembling, I halted.

"As High Champion, it is my duty," he continued in a pompous tone as he unfurled some kind of shiny parchment, "to inform you that you have been charged with a serious offense."

"Charged . . . offense?" My fishtail wobbled beneath me. "There's been a big mistake."

"Affirmative. And you have made it."

"Not me! I didn't do anything. It was her . . . she stole my—"

"Silence!" In a swift movement, he reached into a belt pouch and snapped glowing eel handcuffs on my wrists. "Galena, you are under arrest."

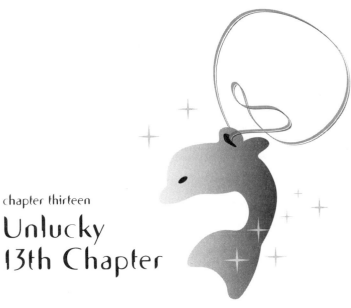

chapter thirteen

# Unlucky 13th Chapter

"But I didn't do anything wrong!" I protested, struggling to shake off the eel-cuffs. But the more I struggled, the tighter they squeezed, the one on my right arm rubbing against the dolphin bracelet.

"Your wicked lies will be your undoing," the chubby mermaid swam forward and pointed at me. "You're a thief!"

"No! I'm innocent!"

"Liar!" she ranted, her words showering forward in large bubbles. "Champion, look at her arm. She's wearing my bracelet! It's proof of her guilt!"

"But it isn't mine—"

"Exactly! It's mine and you had no right to take it. This time you won't slip away so easily. You've been caught in a net of your own lies," the mermaid insisted, her face puffed pink with indignation. The buck-toothed mermaid behind her said nothing, but if her gaze fired lasers, I'd be a fried fish-girl.

"I don't even want this bracelet."

"Well I do!" She grabbed my wrist and yanked hard, but when her fingers touched the bracelet green sparks ignited like fireworks. Zap! She rocketed back and flipped over in a somersault, landing on a squishy green plant. The outraged plant shrieked like a banshee and slapped at the mermaid with thorny fronds.

"Oh poor Fortuna!" the buck-toothed mermaid cried, rushing toward her friend. "Here, take my hand. Ignore Galena. She'll never change."

"I don't need help, Stelleri." Fortuna looked woozy, then shook off the younger mermaid. "But I demand justice!"

"You'll get it," High Champion promised and, at the sound of his voice, my eel-cuffs tightened around my wrists. "Galena has committed her last crime."

"She's a menace," Fortuna said indignantly. "Not only did she steal my bracelet, but I sense magic around her. She must have broken into my scroll library. Lock her away for fifty years."

"Fifty years!" I exclaimed. "But I have to start sixth grade in two months."

"Sixth grade? What is this nonsense?" Fortuna huffed. "More lies!"

"I'm not! My real name is—"

"Enough!" High Champion ordered, gravely stroking his algae-like beard. "Galena, come with me."

I looked around for help, but found only hostility. All this for stealing a bracelet and breaking into a library? What else had Galena done? I had a sinking feeling I was about to find out.

The wondrous world that seemed beautiful a short while ago, now seemed gray and grim. Stark towers of rock blurred by as I was dragged away. I couldn't swim with bound hands, so I floundered behind the High Champion. I vaguely noticed mer-people peering at me from shadows—pointing and staring with hatred. I'd never felt so unpopular in my life!

Before I could wonder where I was being taken, we arrived at the twisted, rusted remains of a sunken cruise ship. It was about the size of a house and looked like it had been through a hurricane. I was whisked up what must have once been a luxurious deck, through a hallway, down a bent hatch, and then shoved into a small steel room.

Clang! A heavy door slammed behind me. The eel-cuffs slid off and slithered away through a tiny slit in the wall. I heard the twist of a key in the lock, then the flutter of fins as my jailers swam away.

Sick at heart, I sank down on a seat. Something underneath me wiggled and squeaked. I shot up, then looked down at a multi-legged green bug scooting away. Gross! And my prison was worse! Slimy algae oozed over cracked tile and seaweed cobwebs slithered around me. There was a sink with a rusted faucet, a crooked rail that had probably been a towel rack, and a small steel toilet with a push-pedal for flushing.

I was locked in a rotting ship's bathroom! Vomit-green ooze clung to the toilet seat and bugs swam in bits of gross dark chunks in the bowl. Yuck! I hoped that Galena's body had a super bladder, because no way was I using *that* toilet!

*Did mermaids even go to the bathroom?* I wondered. I'd gotten used to being underwater, although I really didn't understand it. How did this fishy body function? Curious, I turned my head to study my tail and didn't see a butt-flap. How did the whole mermaid and potty thing work anyway?

Instead of crying, I giggled. Okay, it was weird. But if my only choice was crying or laughing, I'd rather laugh. If I started crying, I might never stop.

"What's so funny?" someone whispered from outside my prison.

I jumped, smacking my head against the towel rack. "Who said that?"

"Me."

"I don't see anyone." I peered around at slimy walls and bugs. Was one of the sea bugs speaking to me?

I was ready to talk to a winged green bug, when a finger poked through the same slit in the wall where the eels had escaped. I felt a rush of love for that little finger. It represented hope. Rescue had arrived!

"Who are you?" I asked.

"Stelleri."

"Oh . . . I remember you," I said, hope sinking. Stelleri was the buck-toothed mermaid who'd glared at me. "What do *you* want?"

"I had to see you."

"Why? So you could gloat because I'm stuck here for fifty years?"

"You could get off early."

"How early?" I asked.

"In forty years—if you're good. Which isn't likely."

"Okay, I get it. You hate me." I sank onto the gross toilet. "Just go away."

"Not until we talk." Her voice trembled.

"So talk. I'm not going anywhere."

"I came to ask . . . ask . . ." There was a pause and tiny, timid bubbles floated through the hole. "Please . . . please return Aunt Fortuna's bracelet."

"Fortuna? Oh, the manatee . . . I mean, gray-haired mermaid."

"Why are you so terrible to Aunt Fortuna? She gave you a home and an apprenticeship. But that wasn't enough—you wanted her bracelet, too. If you have any decency in your heart, give it back."

"I would if I could, but it's stuck." I tugged at my wrist, yet the silver dolphin clung as tight as skin. "I'll need help to get it off. Sorry."

"You're never sorry!" she raged. "This is a trick so I'll unlock the door."

"No, that's not true."

"What do you know about the truth? You've hurt everyone who cared about you. Keep the bracelet. It's no use without Aunt Fortuna's magic anyway."

"Magic?" I lunged toward the hole. But she drew back and I could only see a swirl of purple. "How does it work?"

"Only Aunt Fortuna understands ancient powers."

"Galena must know, too, or I wouldn't be here. She did this to me."

"You did it to yourself. I was a fool to ever think you were my friend."

"We were friends?" I asked, surprised.

"How can you even ask?" she demanded with a sob. "I trusted you . . . but you tricked me. I'll never EVER forgive you."

"I was tricked, too. Please listen to me."

"I listened to you once and look what happened." She gave a ragged sob. "But hurting Aunt Fortuna is even worse."

"I didn't hurt your aunt."

"She's your aunt, too!"

"She is?" I blinked. "You mean we're cousins?"

"We're nothing now!" I heard a slap of fins. "I hope you rot in jail!"

There was a rush of water and silence.

Stelleri was gone.

## chapter fourteen

# More Unlucky than Chapter 13

If I had to be a mermaid, why couldn't I have been a nice one? Instead, I was a thief who betrayed her own family. I knew Galena had stolen from her aunt, but apparently she'd done something awful to Stelleri, too.

No wonder Galena was eager to escape into my human body. While she enjoyed my vacation, I was paying for her crimes. There was nothing I could do except sit on a rusted toilet and wait to be released in fifty years.

I heard a soft tap on the metal wall. "Psst!" someone whispered. "Galena!"

I pressed my face against the wall and peered through the hole.

"Astor!" I cried joyfully. "I'm so glad to see you! Can you get me out of here?"

"Not without a key."

"Break the lock or knock down the door. Do something!"

"I wish I could," he said, swimming close enough so I could see his sad expression. "I am so sorry, Lena."

"You didn't help me when I was arrested. You ditched me," I accused.

"It pained my heart to leave, but no one argues with Champion," he said firmly. "There was no reason to risk being arrested with you, so I bowed out quietly. But I'm here to stay as long as you wish."

"For fifty years?" I asked sarcastically.

"Your sentence won't be that long. The council would never be that cruel to someone so beautiful."

"What does beauty matter?" I demanded, glancing at Galena's image in the jagged remains of a wall mirror. Her violet-blue hair glistened, her creamy skin was luminous, and her large eyes sparkled with tears. I'd rather look like a hammer shark so I could smash out of my prison. Instead I was trapped like a bug in a jar. It made no difference whether I was a butterfly or a slug. Trapped was trapped.

There was silence on the other side of my potty prison. "Astor?" I called out, worried he might have ditched me again. "Are you still there?"

"Yes. But you puzzle me. How can you joke about beauty? You've always been so proud of your appearance."

"Don't you get it yet?" I demanded in exasperation. "I. Am. Not. Galena."

"Is this another trick?"

"No. My real name is Cassie Strange and I'm on vacation with my family. At least I was until Galena used a magic spell to steal my body."

"She would never . . . wait a minute. Did you say a magic spell?"

"Yeah. Something about the moon and tide and powers of the deep."

"Mystic powers of the deep?" he guessed.

"That's it!" I jumped up excitedly. "Can you reverse the spell?"

"No. Only those with centuries of study are permitted to perform magic. Fortuna allows no one in her secret library. But yesterday I heard you reading the spell from a scroll-book. When I asked you where you got the book, you got very angry."

"It wasn't me. It was Galena."

"You do seem different. You sound the same . . . but nicer. You haven't called me Guppy Breath or Fin Fungus."

"Calling names is mean. Why do you want to be with someone who insults you?"

"Because I . . ." Through the tiny hole I saw him blush. "Because I love you."

"Not me," I said softly.

"I care for Galena with my deepest heart. I would do anything for you . . . I mean . . . her." His voice cracked. "You aren't Galena?"

"Bingo. She has my body and I'm stuck with her's."

"It is hard to believe such a wild story. Although my Galena has a wild side and she has studied sorcery. But it would take years of practice to perform such a powerful spell."

"She must be a fast learner."

"Galena is as smart as she is beautiful," he said in this gushing tone that made me want to gag.

"She's also a liar and thief."

"Don't insult her . . . I mean, you . . . Oh! It really is true. You are not my Galena."

"That's what I've been telling you." I rolled my eyes. Dim bulb alert! Galena's beauty must have dulled his brain.

"So it is true," he said sadly. "In that case, I bid you adieu."

"Adieu? Like in goodbye? Wait! You can't leave! You have to help me!"

"I don't even know you. I must go to Galena."

"First get me out of here. Convince the others to let me go and reverse the spell."

"They wouldn't believe me anymore than they believe Galena. She's made many enemies. I'm breaking rules by coming here." Through my peephole, I saw him cup his ear and an expression of horror cross his face. "Oh, no! They're coming!"

"Who?"

"The council."

My pulse jumped with fear. "Council?"

"The Supreme Justice Council. They're coming to give you your sentence."

"How can they sentence me without a trial? I deserve a lawyer and a jury of my peers." I'd read that in a textbook when I'd studied for a Civics quiz. Then my only concern was getting a good grade.

"You have a lawyer," Astor said, glancing around as if searching for a hiding place. "Your Uncle Ballister."

"I have an uncle?"

"Several uncles, but Ballister is the only one still speaking to you. He's Fortuna's husband and your legal guardian."

"The husband of my accuser is my lawyer? That's just great," I said unhappily. "Does he hate me, too?"

"No. He admires beauty and has a strong family loyalty. He will be a good defender. But I have no defender, so I'm jellying out of here. Good luck."

"Yeah." I shuddered. "I'll need it."

Then I sank down on the grimy toilet seat to await my sentence.

chapter fifteen
# Jail Bait

*Thirty or fifty years,* I thought anxiously when I heard the swish of fins approaching. *Either way I'm sunk.*

There was a jangle of a key in a lock, then the door burst open and fresh water (plus tiny fish) rushed into my prison.

A forbidding wall of stern faces filled the doorway. High Champion floated between two very different mermen. The larger one reminded me of a shark with beady eyes and big teeth showing even though he wasn't smiling. And the skinny merman wore wire-rimmed glasses and had a nervous twitch in his right eye.

"Hello, dear niece." The twitchy merman pushed up his glasses and offered me a feeble smile.

"Uncle Ballister?" I guessed, worried by the pity in his gaze. He didn't look very confident. That sinking feeling I'd had earlier grew worse.

"I regret this unfortunate situation," Uncle Ballister said. "But I am confident all will turn out well."

*Easy for you to say,* I thought fearfully. *You're not stuck in a slimy prison.*

"I did my best to reduce your sentence, but it was difficult since you're still wearing the stolen bracelet."

"I can't get it off!" I tried to explain.

"I know. When Fortuna couldn't take it off you, she added a binding spell, so it acts as an alarm if you try to escape." Uncle Ballister's hand shook as he held out a paper toward me. Well, not exactly a paper since we were underwater and paper would get soggy—a shiny flat sheet with writing on it.

"Champion has ruled on your fate and I'm here for support."

"What about him?" I pointed at Shark-face. "Why is he here?"

"To guard dangerous prisoners," the menacing merman answered. "And to carve the guilty tattoo."

"Guilty?" I gulped. "Tattoo?"

"You'll find out." He flashed an evil sharp-toothed grin, like he couldn't wait to sink his teeth into me.

Until now, none of this had seemed completely real—like playing a virtual game. And I expected the magic to reverse so I could return to normal. But reality hit me like a fired torpedo. I was about to be locked up. I didn't know the life span of mer-maids, but fifty years was a long time for humans. And getting tattooed with those sharp teeth would be torture!

Only this morning I'd looked forward to swim-ming, shopping, and hanging out on the beach. And this was supposed to be my vacation!

"My dear Galena," Uncle Ballister said in sorry little bubbles. "Do not despair. I argued your case, explaining that my wife's bracelet would look far more attractive on you."

"That's my defense?" I asked in dismay.

"An excellent strategy," High Champion praised as he stroked his long beard.

"Thank you," Uncle Ballister said, then turned back to me. "After lengthy negotiations, we have come to a decision."

"What?" I gulped.

"A short jail sentence."

"How long is 'short?'" I asked nervously.

"A mere eight months." Uncle Ballister smiled. "Isn't that wonderful?"

Wonderful? I looked around at the algae, rust, and gross lumps in the toilet. Eight hours here was horrible. Eight months would be torture! And I'd miss sixth grade. I'd been framed, but no one believed me—except Astor who had a habit of leaving when things got rough.

"Galena, you should thank your uncle." High Champion narrowed his gaze at me. "Ballister has argued hard on your behalf. Otherwise you would have spent much longer in jail or had to endure severe probation penalties."

Uncle Ballister gently patted my hand. "You will be more comfortable serving your sentence here."

"Let's get on with the tattoo." Shark-face gnashed his teeth.

"No! I don't want one!"

High Champion regarded me sternly. "By accepting the jail sentence, you agreed to wear the guilty mark."

"Then I don't accept!"

"But you have to," Uncle Ballister insisted. "You would hate probation . . . if you survived the horrible penalties."

"Would probation mean getting a tattoo?"

"No," Uncle Ballister answered. "But it would be too humiliating for a delicate flower like you."

"Sign me up! Anything is better than being locked in here and being tattooed. Just tell me what I have to do to get out."

"Are you sure?" Galena's uncle asked in a deathly grave tone.

I nodded.

"As you wish." He gulped in a deep breath and a tiny fish that swam back out his hairy nostrils. "I do hope you won't regret this decision."

*So did I!*

"What do I have to do?"

"Pay for your crime with hard labor," he answered. "You will be bound in servitude to everyone you've wronged."

I was pretty sure servitude meant being a servant, like doing lots of chores and being bossed around. But anything was better than prison and being tattooed by Shark-face.

What could a few chores hurt?

I was about to find out.

## chapter sixteen

# Black Listed

**H**igh Council held out a small scroll the size of a pencil. He uncurled it a few inches and showed me a list written in red ink.

"Galena, these are the complaints filed against you," he explained.

There were five names, with Aunt Fortuna's topping the list:

*Fortuna—Stealing precious jewelry and betrayal*
*Keridwen—Misuse of youngmers*

*Rhea—Sea turtle rampage of kelp plants*
*Albion—Terrorizing a teacher*
*Wollipog—False flirtation*

"Your penalty is to serve one hour with each accuser. You will work at duties befitting of your crimes," High Champion explained.

That didn't sound bad. One hour multiplied by five accusers equaled only five hours. That was tons better than eight months stuck in a jail with a painful tattoo. Why had Galena's uncle made probation sound awful?

"Great!" I agreed eagerly. "I'll do it!"

"Then sentence begins now. You must spend one hour with each name on this list." High Champion gave me an unpleasant smile. He shook the list and it slowly uncurled, rolling down, stretching with names and accusations. It landed on smooth sand and continued to unfold into a huge ribbon of complaints.

When the list finally stopped, it was longer than High Champion's beard.

Five accusers multiplied by hundreds. Impossible! It would take years to work off my probation!

And I remembered how Galena said she wasn't anybody's maid.

Well she wasn't.

But now I was.

chapter seventeen

# A Glimmer of Magic

$M$y first penalty was to work for Keridwen, a tired-looking mermaid with eight active youngmers.

Uncle Ballister escorted me up jagged cliffs to her 18th floor rock dwelling. He warned, "Be patient and polite. No shenanigans like last time."

"Last time?" I questioned.

He gave me a curious look, then said that a few months ago I (Galena) had been assigned the duty of caring for youngmers. But instead of watching them, she'd found an old fishing pole and snagged each youngmer with a hook and tied them up with fishing line. Then she'd left them in a closet and spent the afternoon soaking in a whirlpool.

So I wasn't surprised when Keridwen ordered me to keep away from her youngmers. "Stay in the food chamber," she said as she swam me into a room with a sink and cupboards. "Mop the kelp juice off the cooker and sweep sand from the floor."

I glanced down and saw piles of sand. This was NOT going to be easy.

Uncle Ballister gave me a sympathetic look as he showed me a small hourglass that would mark my time. "When the sand runs out, I'll return to escort you to your next job."

Then he turned over the hourglass and left.

Kelp juice was like gum stuck hard to rock walls. I scrubbed and scrubbed and scrubbed. When that was done, I grabbed a broom and tackled the sandy floor. While I swept, I heard nearby sounds of giggles and singing. Once a small mermaid peeped into my room. I sensed her watching and hoped she'd stay and talk to me. I didn't mind working, but it was lonely. But when I smiled at her, she gasped with fear and swam away.

Sighing, I went back to work.

When the sand was nearly gone, the little mermaid returned. This time I was careful not to look directly at her. Instead I watched from the corner of my eyes. She was a cutie with big brown eyes and red hair in a swarm of tiny braids. When she giggled, she reminded me of Amber, and I ached for home.

"Hi," I said softly without looking up. "What's your name?"

"Linnea," she said after a slight hesitation. "You don't scare me."

"Good. But you scare me."

"That's silly." She giggled.

"Why don't you stay and talk to me?"

"Talk about what?" She sounded unsure, but curious.

"How about pets? Do you have any?"

"No. I'm allergic."

"Too bad."

"I wanted a sea dragon, but Momma said no."

I wasn't sure what a sea dragon was, but it sounded exactly like something Amber would love. I wondered how she was doing with the sea monkeys. Would I ever see them grow three eyes?

"If you really want a pet," I told Linnea, "you should make one."

"How?"

"Draw a picture of a pretend pet. Do you have paper . . . I mean, a scroll?"

She nodded, inching closer to me. "I got ink, too, but I don't draw good."

"I'll help you," I offered.

Minutes later she returned with a scroll and ink (from an octopus!). I told her to start with simple circles. When I finished sweeping sand, I showed her how to link the circles with triangles to make funny animal shapes. It was fun, and for a short while I forgot all my problems. Other youngmers joined in and I helped them make up imaginary pets, too. We were giggling over a seahorse with a starfish face when I heard a shout.

"Get away from my youngmers!" Keridwen, the mother mermaid, glared at me from the doorway.

"I was just showing them how to—" I tried to explain.

But she swooped down like a tsunami and swept her little ones out of the room. Then she pointed to my hourglass. "You've done enough. Now get out!"

The hourglass had emptied and I hadn't even noticed.

When I swam outside, Uncle Ballister was waiting for me. "How did that go?"

"Uh . . ." I crossed my fingers. "Okay."

"Good," he told me. "Now onto Rhea's nursery."

"More youngmers?" I asked hopefully.

"Not that kind of nursery. This is for plants."

He led me away from the rocky dwellings, through a narrow tunnel, and out into a lush meadow of flowing sea plants. Far as I could see, plants swayed in beautiful waves of green, blue, yellow, and purple. A stern mermaid with a flat face and rough webbed fingers shoved a small shovel into my hands.

"Start weeding," Rhea ordered. "I'll be watching you, so you won't get out of work like last time."

"Last time?"

"You know what I'm talking about," she snapped.

"It's been so long," I faltered. "I can't remember exactly . . ."

"Well I'll never forget! You complained because you didn't want to get your hands dirty. You acted like a royal pain in the gills. I tried to be nice and gave you the easy job of gathering kelp. But that was too demeaning for Miss High and Mighty! Instead of gathering kelp, you summoned a herd of sea turtles and they destroyed my entire crop."

"Sorry," I murmured, shocked at Galena's wickedness.

I thought longingly of the community garden back at home. It was one of Mom's environmental projects. Once she brought along a CD player and we danced while we pulled weeds. "This step is the Weed Walk," I'd joked. Then we'd taken home fresh vegetables and made the most delicious salad in the world.

*Mom,* I thought sadly, *Will I ever see you again? Do you even know that I'm gone?*

"Stop daydreaming and get to work," Rhea ordered. "I won't let you ruin another crop. You are the laziest mermaid I've ever met!"

Even though I knew she was criticizing Galena, the insult stung.

*I'll show her,* I vowed. *I'll be the best weeder under the sea.*

Then I set to work, stabbing the shovel into soft sand and yanking out prickly weeds. The weeds scratched my fins, but I didn't slow down. I hummed a favorite song as I worked, imagining that the stabbing and yanking were dance steps. And the hourglass time passed quickly.

I could tell by Rhea's surprised expression that I'd done a good job. She gave me a puzzled look. But she only shrugged and didn't even thank me.

Uncle Ballister was waiting for me.

"So where to now?" I asked, not that I really cared. I was so exhausted I could hardly move. My back ached and my hands were blistered. Eight months in jail was starting to sound good.

But when Uncle Ballister told me where we were going next, I couldn't believe my good luck. After all the hatred and hard work, I finally had hope for finding a reversal spell.

We were going to the most magical dwelling under the sea.

Aunt Fortuna's home.

chapter eighteen

# Giggling Eels

As we swam to Fortuna's, my mind whirled with plans. I needed magic to switch back into my own body. What better place to hunt for magic than in a sea sorcerer's dwelling?

But I had to play it cool. Act obedient while I waited for a chance to search Fortuna's magic scrolls for the spell Galena used on me. Then all I'd have to do is escape, find my way back to Newport through miles of sea, and swap bodies back with Galena.

Impossible! But if I didn't try, I'd spend the rest of my life in fins instead of feet.

When we reached the top dwelling on a high craggy pinnacle, Uncle Ballister turned to me with a grim look. "A word of caution, Galena. Be on your best behavior and do nothing to upset your aunt."

"Don't worry," I told him. "I'm a changed mermaid."

I could tell by the way he rolled his eyes that he didn't believe me.

Uncle Ballister led me through a shadowy doorway. We were so far up from the Heartlight, their dwelling seemed more like a cave than a home. There was only one light tube snaking overhead in a rocky ceiling. Faint shadows played on walls and the sea was as still as a tomb. It reminded me of a haunted house—except we were fathoms deep under the sea.

The dwelling seemed eerie and empty. Fortuna was either gone or avoiding me. Uncle Ballister led me into a vast chamber with circular rock walls and no windows. There were shell cabinets, all locked firmly with glowing eels, and a table overflowing with bottles, jars, shells, and bones. The bones looked human—which made me shudder.

"You're confined to this storeroom. Your job is to scrub grime off those old bottles." Uncle Ballister pointed to a tall pile of grimy bottles in all shapes and sizes. Then he handed me a skinny bristle brush.

I nodded meekly and promised to work hard.

"I'll return in one hour." He flipped over the hourglass and left.

I'd be working hard all right—to find Fortuna's spell scrolls. Once he was gone, I tossed the brush aside and began my search for magic.

Where would a powerful sorceress keep her secret spells? I wondered, as I looked around at all the bottles on a table propped up with two anchors, a shelf full of weird plants, and a wall of rusty cabinets with eel locks.

Cautiously I touched one of the eels and . . . ZAP! A shock wave knocked me backwards. My tail slapped against an anchor, rocking the table, send-ing bottles rattling and rolling in all directions. One bottle sailed off the table. But the good thing about being underwater—the bottle drifted down without breaking.

I whirled back toward the cabinets. "Okay, eels," I said, "there has to be some way to make you move."

The eels didn't flinch.

"So you wanna play tough?" I muttered. "Well, I can, too."

Using the blunt end of my bristle brush, I jabbed an eel. It didn't release, but I swear I heard it giggle. So I jabbed it again. It giggled louder, losing its grasp and sliding right off the handle. Wow! Who knew that eels were ticklish?

I tickled the eels until each one slid away in a fit of giggles.

Then I yanked open the cabinet and found . . . more bottles.

Fortuna's magical library had to be in another room. But would she invite me inside? No chance!

I slumped against the cabinet and covered my face with my hands.

*What happened to my fun vacation?* I thought. *Instead of hanging out on the beach with my best friend, I'm stuck in the wrong body in a wet world that hates me. And I'll never finish my probation. In fifty years, I'll still be working off Galena's penalty.*

Most of all, I missed Mom, Dad, Lucas, Amber, and Rosalie. Would I ever see them again? I'd do anything to have my life back to normal. I'd never argue with Mom and Dad about having to help around the house, I'd offer to run lines with Lucas, be more patient with Amber, and watch all of Rosalie's games.

But none of this could happen without magic.

Sighing, I swam over to the table and picked up the bristle brush.

I don't know how long I scrubbed bottles, when I felt an odd tingle, like a wave of warm lava flowed over me. The hottest spot was under my shell top—where I'd tucked the crystal globe.

Plucking the globe from my top, I stared in astonishment. No longer cold and gray, the pearl-sized globe dazzled like a ball of sunlight. When I stared deeply into it, I glimpsed a mini universe of sky, trees, and buildings.

The magic had returned!

chapter nineteen

# Magic Alive!

**W**hat's making the crystal glow? I puzzled, turning the globe slowly between my fingers. It had only glowed once since leaving Mount Shasta—this morning when I'd walked on the beach. Had that been because I was near Galena? And now I was in her aunt's home—a powerful sea sorceress.

The last time I'd used the globe, it showed my deepest longing. I hoped it would work again and show me a spell to reverse the magic—if one existed!

Tossing aside an ugly blue bottle, I concentrated on the crystal in my palm. "Please show me how to get back home," I whispered.

Images sparkled and whirled. Tiny snowflakes fluttered around a blue sky, then turned to white birds and screeched over a sandy beach. The flock of birds wheeled away and the beach loomed larger. Vague shapes deepened into a clear vision. But instead of seeing a scroll, I saw myself.

Not me, of course, but the imposter who'd stolen my body.

Galena was in a beach shop trying on sparkling rings and bracelets. In the background, I saw my brother Lucas. He wore a green shirt over his swimming trunks and he tapped his foot impatiently.

"Cassie, would you hurry up already?" I heard him complain, "Mom said you could only buy one souvenir, not the whole store."

"Lucas!" I called out to him. "It's Cassie . . . your real sister! Can you hear me?"

Obviously, he couldn't. He leaned against a counter filled with plastic sea toys and frowned at the other me.

Galena still wore the same shorts and T-shirt I'd had on earlier and her shoulders were a rosy shade of fresh sunburn. She glanced into a display mirror as she tried on tiny starfish earrings. "Do you see how perfectly they fit through the tiny ear holes? As if they were created just for me! Everything is so lovely. I want them all."

"Mom only gave us enough money for one souvenir."

"Then I shall need more. Bring some to me."

"Oh, sure," he said, laughing. "I'll go collect all the money lying on the beach."

"Yes, do that," she said with a dismissive wave. "I have shopping to finish."

"Cassie, stop kidding around. Just pick something already."

"It is impossible to choose only one bauble."

"Hurry up or I'll bauble you."

"You speak very rudely," she snapped with a flip of my brown hair. "Go away and I will shop alone."

"Mom and Dad sent me to get you. It's late and we have to go back to the hotel."

She ignored him, admiring a blue rhinestone necklace. "Does this compliment my coloring?"

"Huh?" Lucas narrowed his brows together. "You're being mega weird, Cassie. I'm going outside. You better come, too." Then he turned down an aisle and strode out of the store.

I expected the vision to stay with Galena-AKA-me, but instead it followed Lucas as he sat down on a bench outside the store. He tapped his foot impatiently. Then he reached into a bag and pulled out a pair of pointy plastic teeth.

"Grrr," he said as he slipped them into his mouth. Gnashing the teeth, he snarled ferociously. "Hook's hand was a tasty morsel. I could use dessert."

"Keep away from my hand," someone said with a laugh.

Lucas looked up and we both saw Rosalie.

Her dark hair was pulled back in a thick braid and her T-shirt was grimy with sand. The volleyball game must have ended hours ago, probably while I was weeding kelp. Had her team won or lost? Seeing her made me feel a mix of joy and sorrow. I wanted to be there so badly. But I could only watch and listen while the magic lasted.

Rosalie grinned at my brother, then sat down beside him. "Practicing being a crocodile?" she asked.

"Grrr," he growled and nodded.

"Where'd you get those wicked teeth?"

He pointed to the store and snarled.

"It's a cool store. I was in there earlier with Georgia."

At the mention of Georgia, I felt like growling, too.

Rosalie's expression changed slightly as she glanced toward the store. "So is Cassie in there?"

"Yeah," he nodded. "But beware of weirdness."

"What do you mean?"

"Cassie must have had too much sun." He circled a "crazy" gesture with his hand. "Go tell her we have to leave."

"Me? Talk to Cassie?" Rosalie twisted the end of her braid. "Not a good idea."

"Why?" His fake teeth fell from his mouth into in his hand.

"She's mad at me."

"You have a fight?"

"Not really. She just doesn't like Georgia. She didn't come to my game, and when I saw her on the beach later, she ignored me."

Lucas rubbed his chin thoughtfully. "Know what she did on the way here? Walked right into the street! If I hadn't pulled her back she would have been smacked by a truck."

"No way!"

"She didn't even thank me. Then I caught her doing something worse." Lucas lowered his voice. "Shoplifting."

"No way! Cassie would never steal."

"That's what I thought—until she put on some expensive sandals and headed out of the store without paying."

"You're making that up."

"I know what I saw. What's up with Cassie?" He twirled the fake teeth around his finger and stared off into space. "She hasn't acted this weird since we met Hank in Mount Shasta and explored—" He stopped abruptly and glanced away.

"Hank who?" Rosalie tilted her head curiously.

"Just some kid. Hey, we'd better go." He avoided answering by standing. "Mom and Dad are waiting. If you won't get Cassie, I'll have to."

Lucas disappeared into the store, leaving Rosalie sitting alone on the bench. I thought about how she'd defended me to Lucas, and it felt good. But then I frowned, thinking how she'd gone off with Georgia instead of me.

We'd been friends for so long and always got along. We did lots of fun stuff together, like going on bike rides, making up funny lyrics to songs, creating silly dance steps, and scaring each other during sleepovers with spooky stories.

"Oh, Rosalie," I whispered. "Why did you have to find a new friend? I want things to be like they used to . . . I miss you."

"You miss WHO?"

The voice came from behind me.

Startled, I shrieked and dropped the crystal ball.

Whirling around, I found myself face-to-face with Stelleri.

chapter twenty

# A Brave New Vision

"**W**ho were you talking to?" she repeated in a trembling whisper, as if she was scared of her own voice. It was hard to believe this scrawny mermaid was related to Galena. Stelleri had thin, knobby scales, tangled green-blue hair, and her buck teeth poked out even when her mouth was closed.

"No one." I looked around. "We're the only ones here."

"But I—I heard you," she stammered. "Don't confuse me with your lies. You're up to some new mischief. What?"

"Nothing." I shifted my fin to cover the crystal globe.

But Stelleri followed my gaze, swooped forward, and snatched the globe in a swift movement. I tried to grab it, but all I grabbed was water.

"It glows." She stared down with fascination.

"Give it back!" I demanded.

"The warmth tingles my fingers. Did you steal this from Aunt Fortuna?"

"No! It's mine!"

"You have a habit of claiming everything as yours."

"It really is mine," I said desperately.

Her eyes narrowed and she looked from me to the crystal globe. "Why is this orb so warm?"

"Please give it back."

Stelleri leaned closer to peer inside. "Jumping jellyfish!" She gasped. "It's enchanted!"

I was helpless to do anything but watch as her eyes glazed over and she peered deep within the crystal. I had no idea what she was seeing as her expression grew serious. I had a strong urge to swim away. But my alarm bracelet made that impossible. Besides, where would I go? Surrounded by vast sea, there were no street signs leading home.

Swaying in still water, I waited anxiously while Stelleri peered inside the globe. Finally the glowing dimmed, then faded to darkness. She looked up with a dazed expression.

"Oh my," was all she said. She floated to the table and sank down on the edge.

I sat beside her, fin to fin. "What did you see?" I asked.

"It was so astonishing! This orb is more powerful than sea magic, as if it contains wisdom from another realm."

"It does," I admitted.

"How does it work?"

"It reads your mind and shows your deepest desire."

"I saw a brave mermaid," she whispered.

"Is she someone you know?"

"Yes." She nodded sadly. "Myself, only confident and fearless. I was an explorer, traveling the sea to find plants that offer miracle cures and new magic."

"Sounds great."

"But it isn't true." She gave a wistful sigh. "I'm not brave."

"It took courage to ask me to return your aunt's bracelet."

"But I failed to get it and afterwards I was so nervous I broke out in hives. I'm starting to itch again." She scratched her elbow. "I hate being such a spineless amoeba. If only the vision was true and I really was brave. I long to be an ocean explorer and have the courage to stand up to bullies."

"If you pretend to be brave, you *become* brave," I told her. "Don't ever let a bully know you're scared."

"From now on, I won't," she said, drawing herself up taller and fixing me with a sharp look. "Especially my beautiful cousin."

I knew she meant me, and I felt guilty for all the cruel things Galena must have done to her. There wasn't much I could say, so I just murmured, "I'm sorry."

She regarded me curiously. "You're behaving very strange."

I smiled sadly. "You have no idea."

"Maybe I do." She reached over and put the crystal globe into my hand. "Here, this belongs to you."

"Well, thanks. But I thought you hated me."

"I did. Until I realized something."

"What?" My heart skipped.

"You are not Galena."

chapter twenty-one

# Politeness
# Counts

"**Y**ou're right." I faced Stelleri cautiously, remembering Astor's hostile reaction when he discovered the truth. "Do you mind that I'm not your cousin?"

"Of course not." She gave a whoop that swirled bubbles. "I'm thrilled!"

"Whew, that's a relief. When Astor found out, he ditched me."

"Astor's a kelp-brain. He thinks he's in love with Galena. But I know what my cousin's really like, and I'm glad you aren't her. Who exactly are you?"

141

"Cassie Strange. I'm not even a mermaid."

"Then what are you?"

"Just a normal girl."

"Not so normal now," she said with a hint of a smile. "It must be odd for a land dweller to find herself underwater."

"I can hardly believe it," I admitted. "Just talking to you is so amazing! If I weren't in so much trouble, this would actually be fun."

"Where are you from?"

"I live in California and this is supposed to be my vacation. It's been horrible to be hated and accused of things I didn't do."

"You've been very brave."

"And you're very smart to figure out the switch. What convinced you?" I asked eagerly. "Was it something you saw in the crystal globe?"

"No." She smiled and her buckteeth reminded me of pearls. "It was *you*."

"Me?"

She nodded. "I was shocked to hear that Galena offered to work and was kind to youngmers. At first

I suspected you—I mean, Galena—was plotting something sneaky. But when the youngmers showed me their drawings and I saw all the weeds you pulled, I sensed magic. So I came here to find out for myself."

"How did you figure out I wasn't Galena?"

"It was something you said."

"What?"

"*Please.*" She regarded me solemnly. "Galena is never polite to anyone. Especially me! She treats me like a slave and calls me ugly names. She's rude to everyone and only cares about pleasing herself. She can't be trusted."

"She totally tricked me." Then I explained how Galena pretended to be my friend and stole my body.

"It was terrible of her to leave you to suffer for her crimes. While you work hard, she's having fun," Stelleri said angrily. "That's so unfair."

"That's for sure." I looked around at the piles and piles of bottles. "I'll never finish cleaning."

"Galena hates work. She would have preferred jail."

"Not me. That jail was disgusting!"

"Galena would have conned her way to a better jail. She can talk Uncle Ballister into anything. That's why I was so shocked when you chose probation. Galena would never, EVER willingly agree to work."

"But she's not the one doing it," I said.

Stelleri nodded. "If I were a sorceress like my aunt, I'd switch you back."

"Can you do magic?"

"Only small spells I learned from doing Galena's assignments when she was too lazy to do them herself. To reverse Galena's spell, I'd have to enter my aunt's private library. But that's forbidden."

"What about your aunt?" I asked desperately. "Could she change me back?"

"Of course." Stelleri frowned. "But you would NOT like the results."

"Why not?"

"If my aunt found out you were human, you'd never leave here alive. She had a bad experience with a fisherman and hates all humans."

"What happened?"

"He caught her in his net and locked her in a room on his boat. He'd heard some wild tale about mermaids granting wishes and told her to make him rich or he'd never let her go."

"Can mermaids grant wishes?"

"Not without a spell scroll and special charms like the bracelet you're wearing." She pointed to my wrist. "Since she couldn't give him riches, he forced her to catch fish for him. Every day he chained her and dumped her into the sea, then pulled her back to the boat when she'd gathered enough fish."

"That's horrible! How did she escape?"

"My father found her and brought her scrolls. Once she had her magic, she broke out of the chains and took revenge on the fisherman."

"What did she do to him?" I gulped.

"She turned him into a necklace, so he's now chained around her neck."

"Wow!" was all I could say. Then I gave Stelleri a cautious look and asked, "How do you feel about humans?"

"You're the first one I've met—and I like you."
She flashed her bucktoothed grin. "That's why I've
made an important decision."

"What?"

"I'll help get your body back."

chapter twenty-two
# Prehistoric
# Poop

I swooshed forward and hugged Stelleri. "Thank you!"

"That's something else my cousin would never say." Then she had to leave, but promised to return when she had a plan.

"How will you know where to find me?"

"Easy. Nothing exciting ever happens around here, so we gossip. Everyone will know where Galena is—she's the hottest topic under the sea."

Moments after Stelleri left, my hourglass ran out.

Uncle Ballister returned and led me to huge cages containing odd sea creatures. He pointed to a giant fish in the first cage. "That's a dinkleosteus. The long neck fellow next to him is an elasmosaurus. And the lizard is a kronosaurus."

"These aren't fish—they're dinosaurs!" I exclaimed.

"Shhh," he warned, putting his finger to his mouth. "They may be old, but they still have feelings."

I stared in astonishment. I'd gone on a field trip to an aquarium in 4th grade, but had never seen anything like these freaky creatures.

"Why do you keep them in cages?" I asked curiously.

"To protect them," he answered in a grim tone. "They're the last of their kind. We care for them in hopes of saving them from extinction."

"Wow! Is that a giant shark?" I exclaimed, pointing to an enormous monster that was at least forty feet long.

"That's Meg—short for megalodon." Uncle Ballister reached through the bars and patted the monstrous shark. "She's a real sweetheart."

I saw nothing sweet about her giant mouth with razor-sharp fangs. I swam quickly onto the next cage. Finally something I recognized! "It's a sea turtle. But why is it here—it's not extinct."

"Not yet," he replied with a sad shake of his head. "But within ten years, he could be the last of his kind."

"How sad. So what do I have to do?" I asked. "Feed them?"

"No. Your job is to collect droppings."

"Droppings?" I made a disgusted face. "Like poop?"

"Here's a bucket. Now get to work."

* * *

I hadn't minded watching youngmers, weeding kelp, or cleaning bottles, but collecting poop from prehistoric monsters was downright gross!

When the hourglass turned, I sucked up some courage and started with the smallest, least scary creature: the sea turtle.

"Hey, Mr. Turtle," I said as I opened his cage. "I've come to clean up."

He tucked his head inside his shell.

"Please move aside," I said armed with the bucket and a rake. "I see poop pellets under your floppy feet."

But he didn't budge, and no amount of shoving, pushing, or begging worked. So I dug under him, tunneling to the poop. Then with a swift scoop, my first cage was cleaned.

I eyed the remaining cages—each the size of a garage and parked with a prehistoric predator. If I climbed into those cages, I'd never get out alive. Maybe I could figure out a way to clean from outside the cage . . .

I was tying a rake and a broom together, when Stelleri returned.

Only she wasn't alone.

I glared at her blond companion. "What's *he* doing here?" I demanded.

"Astor offered to help," she answered.

"Him? No way! I don't believe it."

"It's the truth," Astor insisted with a cheery wave. "I am at your service."

"Humph!" I shot Astor a wary glance. I didn't trust him, but I could use all the help I could get— even if his motives were suspect.

"I tried finding the spell Galena used on you," Stelleri said. "I'm afraid it's locked in Fortuna's forbidden library. But I found another spell that should work. It's a temporary spell."

"How temporary?"

"It lasts till sundown."

"How long is that?" I asked with a glance upward. I was pretty sure the sky was above me, but it was completely hidden by endless sea.

"About fifty minutes."

I groaned. "I have to find Galena *and* convince her to return my body in less than an hour?"

"I never said it would be easy. I'll get you to the beach and the rest is up to you."

"But I can't leave or an alarm will sound off." I held up the dolphin bracelet.

"That's why Astor is here."

Astor bowed down to his fins. "Always happy to assist."

"That's not what you said when you found out I wasn't Galena," I reminded.

"I've had a change of heart."

"Couldn't find her by yourself?" I guessed.

"It proves difficult," he admitted. "I know nothing about land dwellers, so I am ready to join forces."

I didn't feel very encouraged. Somewhere above me daylight was fading and time was running out fast. I touched the glittering dolphin eyes on the bracelet. They seemed like spies watching my every move.

"Will your spell stop the alarm?" I asked Stelleri.

"No."

"Then how can I escape?"

"Astor will help."

"Can he get the bracelet off me?"

"Not exactly. But when the spell is done you will no longer be bound by probation." Her bucktoothed grin hinted at secrets.

I glanced over at the cages. I had a feeling the prehistoric shark was eyeing me like I was dessert. Leaving sounded like a great idea.

"Okay. So what now?" I asked, gulping.

"Get ready for another body switch."

"With who?"

She pointed.

## chapter twenty-three
# Switcheroo #2

"ASTOR!" I shrieked loud enough to wake sleeping whales. "But that's impossible! I can't be a boy!"

"Why not?" she asked with a shrug.

"Because he is . . . and I'm not . . . I mean, because it's just weird!"

But she was already chanting the spell and it wasn't like I had a better plan.

*Windswept beaches, briny sea*
*Swirling secrets, mystery.*
*Starfish dance and dolphins leap,*

*Powers old, within your deep*
*Souls exchange in bright sunlight*
*To be returned when day comes night.*


Suddenly I was swept up in a tornado. Violet-blue hair swirled around me, binding me like a mummy. My head spun dizzily and everything blurred. I cried out, but my voice was lost in the whirling waves.

Then everything stopped—and I felt different.

Strong, bold . . . and bare.

With a glance down, I shrieked. I used to worry about being flat-chested, but never THIS flat. My shoulders were wider, muscles bulged in my arms, and there was stubble on my chin. Yuck!

I was Astor. But even weirder—Astor now looked like Galena. And when he gasped, he sounded just like her, too.

Astor-as-Galena twirled violet-blue hair around his (her?) fingers. "This is amazing."

"Tell me about it!" I flexed my arms, watching hard muscles roll like an army on my arm. "I've never been a guy before."

"And I've never been a mermaid. I even sound like a girl."

"I sound like a walrus," I complained.

"Don't insult my voice."

"Cut it out you two." Stelleri stretched her arms out between us. "This is only temporary. When the sun sets, Astor will return to his own body and—"

"And I'll still be Galena," I finished.

"Not if we find the real Galena first and she changes you back."

"I hope so."

Astor-Galena admired his new body. "Look at me! I'm beautiful."

"Yes, you are," Stelleri said with a sad smile.

"If I can't be with Galena," Astor added, "*being* her is the next best thing."

"Hold that thought," I said with a chuckle as I handed him a bucket heaping with turtle droppings. "Enjoy being Galena."

I heard his soft, new, beautiful voice shriek as I left with Stelleri.

Swimming in my new body was incredible. My arms were stronger and more powerful. Being a mer-guy had its advantages.

Stelleri and I broke through waves. For the first time in hours I breathed in fresh air. It made my throat itch a little and I coughed.

"There's the cove where Galena stole my body," I said, pointing.

"Do you want to go there?" Stelleri asked.

"No. Galena is with my parents back in the hotel by now." I glanced at the setting sun. "I need legs to get her."

"That's beyond my abilities."

"So what's your plan to find her?"

"Coming here was my plan," she admitted with a frown.

"Oh," I said, hopes sinking.

"Don't you have any ideas?"

"Nope. With fins instead of feet, we can't crawl or hop to the hotel. We need wheels. Can a mer-maid pedal a bicycle?"

Stelleri shook her head. "But it would be fun to try."

"We don't have a bike anyway. Not even a skate-board. It's hopeless; we're stuck here." I slapped the ocean. "There's no way we can get to Galena."

"If only we could get her to come to us."

"She'll never do it," I said. "She won't risk get-ting near the sea."

"Unless we trick her—like she tricked us."

I looked at Stelleri curiously. "You never have told me what she did to you."

"I don't speak of it." Stelleri glanced away.

"It can't be that bad. I didn't see your name on the list of complaints."

"She's my cousin and I don't rat on family." Then she pushed ahead and I had to flap my fins fast to catch up to her.

We had floated close to the beach and hid behind a bobbing orange buoy. The only people on the beach were a young couple walking close together, a woman wading in the waves while talking on a cell phone, and a man walking a basset hound.

"Stelleri!" I exclaimed suddenly. "I have an idea!"

chapter twenty-four
# SOS Call

Once Stelleri heard my idea and agreed it might work, we sprang into action.

We left the safety of the buoy. Stelleri swam ahead and I followed underwater. It was easier to breathe under water anyway. When I was close to the shore, I ducked behind a large rock.

All was calm on the beach. Sea gulls wailed and a swift wind chased discarded papers across warmed sand. The lovey-dovey couple wandered back towards the hotels; the dog took off running, causing his owner to sprint in pursuit; and only the woman on the phone remained.

"Perfect," I murmured.

Then there was a loud splash and a shrill scream.

Stelleri popped out of the water and floundered as if she were drowning. "Help! Help!" she cried, only her head and arms visible above foaming waves. "I can't swim!"

Phone-woman whirled with a gasp. "I'll call for help!" she offered quickly.

"Not . . . enough . . . time," Stelleri gasped, treading water.

"But I can't swim very well!" the woman called, panicked. "There's no lifeguard!"

"Help!" Stelleri bobbed underwater, then sputtered when she came back up. "Can't . . . hold on . . ."

"Oh, no!" the woman exclaimed, looking around frantically. "I'll get someone! Wait for me!"

"Can't . . ." Stelleri raised her arms and slipped underwater. "Too weak . . ."

"Don't drown!" The woman kicked off her shoes and dropped her phone. Then she rushed forward in the surf.

I had to hand it to Stelleri. She played her part well (Lucas would be impressed!). When the woman waded too close, Stelleri pulled away and drifted a little further down the shore. I felt sorry for deceiving the woman, but my entire future was at stake!

When Stelleri lured the woman far enough away, I swam to the edge of the surf and wobbled across the sand. Like a worm, I inched forward on the wet sand, pushing forward with my powerful tail. When I was near the woman's discarded belongings, I stretched out my arm. But I was still two feet away, and without feet, that distance seemed like miles.

As I was doing the worm-crawl again, a wave crashed over me. The rushing water surged me forward and contact! My fingers closed over my prize.

Success! I had the cell phone!

Holding the phone above water, I rode another wave back into the sea.

Now for part two of my plan: calling my family.
I had three major problems to overcome:

1. I didn't know the hotel number.

2. No one knew I was in trouble.

3. I sounded like a walrus.

After some thought, I figured out a plan. Instead of calling the hotel, I'd call Dad's cell phone. It was his work line and I was only allowed to use it in an emergency. Being half-fish definitely counted as an emergency.

Of course it would be impossible to convince Dad I was in trouble with the other me around. So I planned to ask for Lucas. Before Dad could get mad about Lucas giving out his private number, I'd say I had an urgent message from Lucas's acting teacher.

Lucas already suspected something odd was going on. So he should believe me. If he needed proof about my identity, I'd mention our secret adventure in Mount Shasta. My brother was part goofball and genius—the perfect combo to help.

I pushed in the phone numbers and waited . . .

After three rings, I grew anxious. Why wasn't anyone answering? Didn't Dad have his phone turned on or had he left it in the car again? I couldn't exactly leave a voice mail message!

When someone answered—I almost sank with shock.

"Rosalie!" I exclaimed. "I didn't expect you. Where's Dad?"

"Who is this?" she asked suspiciously.

"It's me!" Then remembered I sounded like Astor. "I mean . . . I'm a friend of Lucas's."

"Do I know you?"

"Uh . . . not exactly. But Lucas told me who you were. Is he around?"

"Nope."

"Can you find him? It's really important."

"I'm doing something important, too. Babysitting Amber. I can't leave, but I'll take a message."

"No! That won't work . . . I mean . . . why are you babysitting anyway? Isn't that Cassie's job?"

"She's missing. Her parents and Lucas are out looking for her."

"Missing? But she can't be gone or I'll never be able to—" I slapped my hand over my mouth.

"Able to what?" Rosalie demanded. "I thought you wanted Lucas."

"Yeah. I really, really need to talk with him."

"Something fishy is going on. Who exactly are you?"

"I'm . . ." Lies darted in and out of my mind. But I didn't want to lie to Rosalie. We'd been best friends for a long time, and that meant a lot.

So I took a deep breath and a big risk.

I decided to tell her the truth.

chapter twenty-five

# Rose Bush and Cassandruff

"Rosalie, do you remember when I . . . when Cassie told you she was going to tell you an important secret?"

"That's private between us. What do you know about it?"

"Everything."

The suspicious level rose in her voice. "Why would Cassie tell you her secret?"

"She didn't tell me . . . I mean . . . this is hard to explain."

"What? . . . can't hear . . . you say . . . something?"

"Darn! We're losing the signal. Can you hear me?"

"Yeah, but it's faint. What do you want? Is this some kind of prank?"

"No!" I tried to think of something convincing to say.

"I don't believe you. I'm hanging up."

"You Brainless Rose Bush, don't you dare hang up!"

"What did you call me?" she demanded in astonishment.

"Rose Bush. Just like you call me Cassandruff. And if you don't listen to me I'll flush your patottle down the toilet just like you did to my wongbang!"

"That was an accident, and no one knows except Cassie."

"Bingo. That's what I'm trying to tell you. I am Cassie."

"Don't be crazy. You're a guy."

"I've changed a lot since this morning."

"Nobody changes that much."

"They do with magic." I heard static on the line and was afraid of losing the connection, so I spoke fast. "I know I sound different, but I'm the same Cassie who made chicken soup and sandwiches for you when you were sick and who dyed my hair green last St. Patrick's day."

"A really gross puke-green," she said with a chuckle. "It got on Cassie's ears."

"My ears. You said I looked like a leprechaun from Mars. Then you laughed so hard you wet your pants."

"Did not! I spilled my soda."

"You weren't drinking any soda."

"Well, I spilled something . . . oh my!" She gasped. "You really are Cassie! But it isn't possible!"

"I can prove it if you meet me in the cove behind the hotel."

"I can't leave when I'm watching Amber. She said she was washing her hands, but she's been in the bathroom for over fifteen minutes."

*Sea monkeys,* I thought with a smile. But I'd promised to keep Amber's secret, so I didn't mention this. Instead, I told Rosalie to bring Amber if she had to and meet me behind the hotel ASAP. As she was agreeing, the phone died.

Lightly tossing the phone back on the beach, I hurried to the cove behind the hotel. I pulled myself onto a rock, keeping my tail underwater. It was only a few minutes before Stelleri showed up.

"That was a close call!" Her cheeks were flushed and she was grinning. "A man walking a dog was coming over and the woman almost swam out to save me. But I called out that I was fine and didn't need help. Then I swam away."

"You were great!" I made room on my rock for her to sit beside me. "Thanks."

"Did you call your brother?"

"Yes and no." As I was explaining what happened, I heard a sound and looked up to see Rosalie making her way along the beach to the cove. I was surprised—and pleased—to see she was alone.

"Over here!" I called out, waving my muscular arm.

Rosalie crossed over boulders to reach a rocky shelf. She knelt down and stared with a look of amazement. "Cassie?" she asked in disbelief.

"Yeah." I raised my hand. "But where's Amber? Aren't you babysitting."

"I was, only her parents . . . *your parents* came back. They were checking to see if I heard from you. Of course I didn't tell them anything . . ." Her voice trailed off and she stared in shock. "You . . . you really are a mermaid."

"She's a mermaid." I gestured to Stelleri. "I'm a merguy. This body is a rental, but inside I'm Cassie."

"I'm seeing things." Rosalie put her hand to her forehead. "This isn't real."

"I wish it weren't." I slid off the rock and swam over to my friend. I could tell she was confused. And who could blame her? I was shocked when I first saw a mermaid, too.

"Rosalie," I spoke softly, "I know this is hard to believe, but I'm Cassie."

"You're a guy and you have a tail!"

"Welcome to my weird world." I sighed. "You have no idea what I've been through today."

She rubbed her eyes. "People don't just turn into mermaids . . . I mean . . . merguys. Prove that you're Cassie."

"Ask me something."

"What's your middle name?"

"Lynnelle."

"And the name of your dog?"

"Honey. Our cat is named Trixie. But don't quiz me on Amber's zoo of pets—that would take too long."

"Then tell me something only Cassie knows." She glanced at Stelleri uneasily, then lowered her voice so only I could hear. "In third grade, I had a secret crush on someone older. Who?"

"Your soccer coach," I whispered. "You sent him a secret valentine and didn't sign it. When he saw the return address, he thought it was from your mother and sent her flowers."

"Mom figured it was a mistake. But she went around smiling for a week," Rosalie finished with a giggle. Then she sobered as she gazed down at my golden head and handsome body. "Oh, Cassie. What happened to you?"

"I was tricked by a mermaid named Galena. She put a spell on me and switched into my body."

"So she looks like you?"

"Exactly."

"So that's why Cassie has been acting weird. Lucas caught her shoplifting."

"She's a liar and a thief. There's no time to explain, but if I don't switch back soon I'll be stuck in the sea forever."

"Yikes!" Rosalie cried. "What can I do to help?"

"Convince Galena to meet with me."

"But I don't know how to find her."

"Look behind you," a voice rang out from a large rock near Rosalie. "I'm already here."

And I saw myself—well, my body anyway—perched on a rock.

"My how you've changed Astor . . . or should I say, Cassie." Galena leaned forward with a scowl. "Stelleri, what are you doing so far from home? It's dangerous to leave our world."

"That didn't stop you," her cousin accused.

"But unlike you, nothing frightens me. I've been having loads of fun as a human. I love having legs and shopping! Look at my new baubles!" She held out her (my!) hand. There were two sparkly rings and a pink rhinestone bracelet.

"Galena, be reasonable," Stelleri said, swimming closer. "You don't belong above water. Undo the spell and come *home*."

"Home! Where I'll be arrested and sent to jail? Where no one treats me with the proper respect? I'm never going back."

"I'll tell everyone you're a fake," Rosalie threatened.

"Go ahead. Who's gonna believe you?" She gave a wicked laugh. "Do not make me angry or Cassie will be sorry."

"I'm already sorry I trusted you," I said bitterly.

"Don't let her scare you," Stelleri added. "Galena's magic only works in the sea. She can't harm you."

"Who needs magic?" She leaned closer so I was facing myself. "Ever heard of someone named Sebastian Mooncraft?"

"Mooncraft? He's a rival of my dad's." I gagged on seawater. "What do you know about him?"

"He's in Newport."

"Here!"

"He heard about a mermaid siting and plans to capture a mermaid for his TV show. You were very careless to let humans see you."

I cringed, remembering the little boy and guys in scuba gear. No wonder Mooncraft had shown up. He'd do anything to improve ratings for his trashy cable show *Mooncraft's Miracles*.

"You will return to the sea and never show yourself near shore again. Or I'll make sure Mooncraft gets his mermaid . . . or merman," Galena threatened.

Then she spun around on my legs and walked away.

chapter twenty-six

# A Soggy Future

Galena had won.

I couldn't risk being captured by Mooncraft.

There was nothing I could do except return to the deep ocean.

Rosalie begged me to stay, but I shook my head. When we said good-bye, I tried hard not to cry. I was sure I'd never see her again.

*I'm doomed to be a mermaid,* I thought as Stelleri and I swam back.

The hourglass had only a few grains left of sand when we returned to Astor. His silky braid was mussed and there were scratches on his (Galena's) arms. He held a bucket full of monster droppings.

"Thank heavens you're back!" he exclaimed when he saw us. "Do you have any idea how hard it is to clean up after a megalodon? I'm lucky to be alive!"

"But you're still beautiful," Stelleri teased.

"I no longer care about beauty."

"I don't believe it." Stelleri's eyes widened.

"This experience cured me." He glanced at the cages and shuddered. "Silky hair gets in the way and hurts when it tangles. I will be happy never to see this body again."

"So you aren't going after Galena?" I asked.

"No. I never want to see her—" His voice cracked and he choked out, "I'm changing!"

"Me, too," I tried to say only my voice was swept away in an electric blue whirlpool. Waves swirled and I twirled in a tornado of energy.

Then it was over and I was facing Astor.

"I'm me again!" he whooped.

"But I'm still not me," I said in a dull, discouraged tone. "I'm Galena."

"Better you than me." Astor flexed his muscles and caressed his blond hair. "I am glad that's over and now I bid you adieu. Good luck and goodbye."

He swam away so fast he stirred waves and my long, violet-blue hair slapped my face. I frowned at the scratches on my arm. They stung a little. But it hurt worse knowing I was stuck with Galena's body.

Stelleri guessed what I was thinking. "It's not that bad."

"It's worse." My heart ached as I thought of Rosalie, my family, and the home I'd never see again.

"You'll learn to like being a mermaid."

"Not when everyone hates me."

"Not everyone." She squeezed my hand. "I like you. And I'll help you break the spell."

"Thanks," I said. But I knew it was hopeless. What could she do? She had no power over Galena and she was too timid to sneak into her aunt's scroll library.

Stelleri swam away seconds before her uncle returned.

Uncle Ballister scowled when he saw the scratches on my arm. "I told the Council your penalty was too severe. I won't stand for this outrage."

He was still grumbling when he left me at my last job for the day. It was easy enough. All I had to do was count out fish eggs and sort them by size.

I was up to 3,501 eggs when my time ran out. I heard a swish of fins and was surprised to see Stelleri instead of her uncle.

"Why are you here?" I asked.

"I offered to take you back."

I made a face. "To that awful, stinky jail?"

"Is that where you want to go?"

"Of course not!"

"Then I'll take you someplace nicer." Her buck-toothed smile grew wide. "Uncle Ballister is a softie and talked the Council into giving you a day off. So you're coming home with me."

"Wow! That's great!"

"It's just the beginning." Her toothy smile flashed. "You may think your old life was better, but I'll show you around my world. Mer-girls can have fun, too."

chapter twenty-seven

# Sleeping Over
# Under the Sea

That's when things improved.

I was still stuck in Galena's body. But I wasn't as miserable.

Stelleri lived in this cool third-story cave. Her walls were painted aqua blue and had a great collection of odd-shaped coral. We sat on a sponge couch and she taught me a game like jacks. We flipped seed pods with our tails, then caught them in a net before they floated away. She won: 27 to 5.

Afterwards, we snacked on sea fruit and a spongy plant that tasted like popcorn. Then she unfolded a scroll album and showed me drawings of herself as a youngmer. She was so cute with rosy cheeks and tiny teeth. In one picture she played dress-up with another youngmer with violet-blue hair and large teeth.

I studied this picture, a suspicion growing in my mind.

"Galena tricked you into a switch, too," I guessed. "That's the awful thing you didn't want to talk about."

"Yes," Stelleri said sadly. She reached up to her mouth. "She was always beautiful, except for her teeth. I was always homely, except for my smile. I knew she was jealous; still, I was shocked when she stole my smile."

"Why didn't your aunt or uncle make her switch back?"

"They didn't notice," she said sadly. "And I was so hurt, I never told them."

"That's so unfair! You should tell them."

"I can't. It would only upset everyone."

"If you don't, I will."

"No! Please, don't."

Her tone was firm, so I didn't argue. Still I thought it was unfair.

Stelleri and I stayed up late. We talked, played games, and giggled. It was just like a sleepover. The next morning, Stelleri surprised me with breakfast (some kind of fish pancake) in bed.

"Hurry and eat!" she said excitedly. "We have lots of places to see."

"But I can't go very far." I pointed to my dolphin bracelet snug around my wrist. "The alarm will go off."

"Not today," she told me. "Come on!"

And that began an amazing morning.

Stelleri and I carried round tubes filled with Heart-light gasses like glow sticks. We swam away from the cave dwellings and deep into the sea. She took me to a huge castle of coral, a tunnel where the sea swooshed down like a water slide, and to a private sandy cover. We flopped in shallow water and made a sand castle decorated with beautiful seashells.

She gave me some tips for swimming faster, and then we had races. I was amazed how fast we swam. Dolphins couldn't even keep up. We swam north until we reached the rusty steel skeleton of a sunken ship. Waves crashed around the shadowy wreck. "It's from a ship called the Peter Iredale and crashed like a hundred years ago," Stelleri explained.

When we returned to her cave, I was tired in a good way.

"I had a great time," I told her as I leaned back on a sponge couch.

"I told you mer-girls have fun."

"You're right," I said with a laugh.

"When your penalty is over, you'll like living here. Life is easy under the sea. We have few needs and food is plentiful."

"It is nice," I admitted.

"It's wonderful and I'm so glad you're here."

The way she said that made me uneasy. She'd promised to help me get back into my own body. But did she really mean it?

While Stelleri left to do some chores for her aunt, I pulled out the crystal globe. I closed my eyes and concentrated. When I opened my eyes, the globe sparkled with images.

"What does grounded mean?" I heard my own voice whine.

Peering closer to the globe, I saw Galena in my parents' hotel room. She sat on a chair facing my parents with her arms folded across her chest.

"You will not leave this room all day," Dad ordered.

"Cassie, I'm disappointed in you," Mom added. "You scared us last night. Why were you at that bus station? What were you thinking?"

Galena refused to meet their gazes. When Mom reached out to touch her shoulder, she flinched. "Ouch!"

"You have a bad sunburn," Mom said. "Why didn't you put on sunscreen?"

"Sunscreen?" she murmured.

I almost felt sorry for Galena. She was finding out that being human didn't mean she could do what she wanted. She needed money to buy baubles and she needed permission to leave the hotel.

The screen faded and when it cleared, I saw Rosalie and Lucas in my hotel room.

Lucas had a stunned expression. "So she's not my sister?" he exclaimed.

"It's hard to believe, but it's true." Rosalie twisted her long braid. "I had to tell someone and something Cassie—the real Cassie—said made me think you'd understand."

"I don't understand, but I do believe you."

"Really?" She brightened.

"Sure. Cassie is like a magnet for weird stuff. And she's been acting goofy. Of course, I never guessed she'd turned into a mermaid, but it makes more sense than her stealing from a store."

If I weren't holding the crystal, I would have applauded my brother. Bravo!

"So how do we help her?" Lucas was asking.

"I don't know. The only way is with magic and we don't have any."

"But the fake Cassie does," Lucas said with a thoughtful pause. "We have to get her to return my sister before we leave for home."

"She'll never change back. She wants to have fun as a human."

"So we ruin her fun." Lucas's dark eyes twinkled. "Here's what we're going to do . . ."

It figures the image would end just then. Like the globe had a warped sense of humor. But it had shown me enough. And I couldn't wait to tell Stelleri.

But when she returned from her aunt's, she had news of her own.

Aunt Fortuna had guessed something was different with Galena, so she conjured up a powerful spell to reveal my secrets.

She knew I was a human in disguise.

*And she was angry.*

## chapter twenty-eight
# Escape!

Any mermaid vengeful enough to wear a fisherman for jewelry was not someone I wanted mad at me.

Stelleri was clearly worried, too.

"There is no choice," she spoke sadly. "You have to leave."

"Won't they come after me?"

"Not right away." She pointed to the dolphin bracelet. "Fortunately, the alarm is shut off and my aunt trusts me to guard you."

"She won't trust you if you help me escape."

"Too late. I've done something far worse." Stelleri reached behind her and showed me a large rolled scroll.

"What's that?"

"My aunt's spell scroll. I entered her private library and stole it." Her hands shook. "It has the spell to reverse Galena's switch."

My jaw dropped. "You broke the law for me?"

She nodded gravely.

"Aren't you afraid of getting into trouble?"

"I'm more worried about protecting you. I don't want my aunt to hurt you."

"Thanks." I balanced on my tail and hugged her. "That's the bravest thing anyone ever did for me."

"You're calling me . . . brave?"

"The very bravest!"

Her smile widened into the most beautiful grin under the sea.

* * *

I kept looking over my shoulder, expecting to see someone after me. But I saw no one. Maybe the

Council didn't know I'd escaped. Still, I moved cautiously.

When Stelleri and I reached the cove, we hid in the shadows of jutting rocks and talked underwater so no one would overhear.

"Galena must wear the bracelet when I chant the spell," Stelleri explained.

"But it won't come off." I tugged on my wrist.

"It will now. While looking for the switching spell, I found a spell that will release your bracelet. It was short and easy to memorize."

"Great!" Eagerly, I held out my wrist where the dolphin eyes glittered. "So get it off."

"Just a minute while I change my voice. It's in dolphin speak, so you may want to cover your ears." She closed her eyes and started to make high-pitched noises. There weren't any words, more like shrieks and clicks.

My wrist tingled and the silver bracelet began to move. The dolphin wiggled, then leaped from my arm to Stelleri's outstretched palm.

"That's so much better!" I exclaimed, rubbing the red circle mark on my wrist. "Thanks!"

"You're welcome." She tucked the bracelet inside her shell top. "Now if we can just get the bracelet on Galena."

"That won't be easy."

"Nothing ever is," Stelleri said with a sigh.

Unfortunately, neither of us had any good ideas.

We were trying to figure out a way to slip the bracelet on Galena while she was asleep, when Stelleri suddenly tensed. She pointed to the shore. "Someone's near."

I shaded my eyes from the bright sun with my hand as I looked. Then I gave a joyful whoop and called out, "Rosalie!"

"Cassie!"

We met each other halfway in the foamy surf. Seawater drenched her sneakers, but she didn't seem to notice. I couldn't stand, so she bent down to hug me. "Oh, Cassie! I've been so worried!"

"Me, too!"

"Are you okay?"

"Yeah . . . for now anyway." I glanced around nervously. "Have you seen Mooncraft?"

She nodded. "He's staying at the fancy hotel next to ours that looks like a castle. Your dad is really mad, too. He said Mooncraft was crazy to believe mermaids were real."

"Crazy, huh?" I teased with a flip of my tail.

I heard a gasp from behind Rosalie.

"It's just Lucas," Rosalie said quickly. "I hope it was okay to bring him."

"Good idea."

"I wasn't sure if you'd mind. He knew something was going on, so I told him everything. Maybe he can help."

"I can use all the help I can get."

My brother stepped out. When he saw two mermaids his eyes widened. "Wow! I thought I knew what to expect . . . but . . . WOW!"

We all laughed. But I noticed Stelleri covered her mouth with her hand as if she was ashamed of her teeth.

Hanging onto a rock, I explained my idea. When I finished, I told Rosalie and Lucas it was their job to bring Galena to the beach.

"She won't go anywhere with us," Rosalie bit her lip. "Not after what we did."

"Yeah." Lucas pushed his windblown hair from his face. "She's mad at us."

"It was your idea to tell her the honey was a sunburn lotion," Rosalie said.

He chuckled. "She was a sticky mess."

"Flies started buzzing around and when she swatted they them stuck to her skin. She wanted to take a shower," Rosalie added, "but I told her water on a sunburn would make her skin fall off."

"You didn't!" I burst out laughing.

"We did," Rosalie said proudly. "When your mom ordered her to wash off the honey, Cassie . . . I mean, Galena . . . screamed. It took forever for your mom to convince her take a shower."

"It won't be easy to fool her again, but it's not impossible." Lucas pulled out his crocodile teeth and twirled them on his thumb. "I know a way to get her to the beach."

"Tying her up and kidnapping her?" I guessed.

"Nothing that drastic. All I need is the bracelet."

"Are you sure you can get her to wear it?" Stelleri asked.

"If anyone can trick her, it's Lucas." I looked at my brother curiously. "So what's your plan?"

"Bribery."

He plopped the teeth into his mouth.

Then he grinned like a wicked crocodile.

chapter twenty-nine

# Lies, Cameras, and Action!

"So what do you think is happening?" Stelleri asked for the zillionth time. I thought I was impatient, but Stelleri was worse!

"I don't know," I told her again.

"Check your magic crystal."

"I will if they don't show up soon."

"It's been over an hour."

"How can you tell? You don't wear a watch."

"Mermaid intuition." She circled around, then pointed toward the shore. "Galena and Lucas are here!"

"But not Rosalie," I said uneasily.

"Hurry! Hide!" Stelleri exclaimed.

My heart thumped anxiously as we dove behind a large rock.

"This is an odd place to rehearse a play," Galena told my brother.

"The scene takes place on the beach," Lucas said. "You're playing the part of Wendy and I'm the crocodile."

*Hmmm,* I puzzled, *since when did she become Wendy?*

I was surprised to see Galena wearing my mother's silk robe over a pair of jeans. Her hair was swept back in curls and she wore the kind of cheap jewelry you could buy at a dollar store. There were at least four necklaces, rings on every finger, dangling earrings, and purple bangles on her arms.

"I am a skilled actress," Galena went on in her regal tone. "My memory for lines will amaze you."

"You'll make a great Wendy. Thanks for helping out."

"Anything is better than cleaning the beach. I am much relieved to escape that drudgery. Although I find it odd that Rosalie went in my place. I don't know why she would be nice to me."

"She's your best friend, isn't she?"

"Er . . . of course." Galena recovered quickly and asked, "So, where is this new bauble you promised me?"

"Right here." Opening a bag, Lucas lifted out a wide rhinestone bracelet.

"Ooh! Lovely!" Galena grabbed for it.

"Let me put it on for you, fair lady," Lucas said with a gallant sweep of his arm. Geez! He was such a ham.

Stelleri gnawed her lip anxiously. "That's not the right bracelet," she whispered.

I noticed the bracelet was unusually wide and bulky. "Maybe it is."

"Oh . . . in disguise?"

"I think so."

My brother fastened the bracelet on Galena, then handed her a paper. "Here's your part."

"Only five lines?"

"It's a very important scene, where the crocodile tries to enchant Wendy. This is a special version of *Peter Pan* created just for Wendy."

"Splendid!" She beamed. "Then I approve."

"The evil crocodile plans to kidnap the beautiful Wendy so Peter will come to the rescue."

"When do I say my lines?"

"Not until I tell you. While the crocodile creeps on the shore, you must lie quietly on this blanket and pretend to be asleep."

She slid gracefully to the blanket. "Like this?"

"Exactly! You're really talented!"

"I know." She fluttered her lashes then closed her eyes in fake slumber.

Lucas tiptoed over to the shore. He gestured for us to join him.

"Stelleri, you're on," he said quietly. Bending down, he whispered in her ear. She listened, nodding and smiling.

"What did he say?" I asked Stelleri when Lucas checked some papers and walked halfway back to Galena.

"It's time for the switch."

"I sure hope this works."

"If it does, you might lose your crystal globe." She swayed gently in the waves. "Would you like me to keep it for you?"

"Good idea," I murmured, handing it over.

Lucas called out to Galena, "The crocodile creeps out of the water and approaches the beautiful Wendy . . . action!"

Then he started singing in a raspy crocodile voice. The words made little sense: pirate jargon mixed with nonsense like "shiver me timbers and croco-roco-dile a nananan ding dong."

Stelleri unfurled the scroll. When Lucas paused in his song, she took over, doing a perfect imitation of his crocodile voice. Only instead of uttering nonsense, she said the first line of the spell. Then Lucas continued with his silly song. The switch was so smooth, if I hadn't been watching, I would never have known.

Each time Lucas paused, Stelleri growled another line of the spell.

Unaware, Galena lay still on the blanket. Either she really was a good actress or she was actually asleep. My vote was for asleep. Was she dreaming of shopping malls full of endless shoe stores?

When Stelleri uttered the final line of the spell, about summoning a sea switch, Galena stirred. Her eyes popped open and she lifted her head. She started to turn around, but it was too late. Silver-blue lightning flashed, and she shrieked as her legs became a floppy fish tail.

Dizzy lights flickered in my head. The spell was changing me, too. My skin tingled and noise roared in my ears. Waves knocked me over, and I tumbled, spinning and sinking down. Water choked my lungs. I gagged and kicked. I couldn't breathe and was drowning . . .

There was a tug on my arm, and I was yanked out of the water.

"Stelleri!" I cried gratefully as she swam me back to shore. "Thanks!"

"You belong on the land."

I reached down and touched my legs. "Yes! I'm back."

"And so is my cousin," Stelleri groaned.

I watched the outraged violet-blue-haired mermaid squirm on the sand. "Where did my legs go? I can't walk!"

"As it should be—you *are* a mermaid," Stelleri said smugly. "Welcome back to the sea, Cuz."

"Betrayer!" Galena shrieked. "My own cousin tricked me with magic!"

"I can't take all the credit," she said proudly. "My friends helped."

"I hate you! I hate you *all*! How could you do this to me?"

"Easy," Lucas said with a chuckle.

He nodded at me and I knew exactly what he was thinking. Together we reached for Galena, each taking an arm. Then we walked over to the water and dropped her.

Plop! Splash!

"How . . . How dare you!" Galena sputtered.

"You're lucky I didn't do worse." Lucas bared his croc teeth. "Don't mess with my sister again, you sea witch!"

"Vile human! I'll turn you into a sea slug!" Galena threatened. "I'll send an army of sharks to chomp your pathetic human bones and devour you!"

"Aunt Fortuna won't allow you to use magic again," Stelleri said with an amused smile. "Face it, Galena, you can't scare us."

"But you should be scared." I smiled wickedly. "Enjoy probation."

"Probation? What probation?"

You'll find out," her cousin said. "You better hurry back before you get into worse trouble."

Galena balled her fists as if she wanted to hit someone. Instead, she flipped her tail and started to swim away.

We watched her swim beyond the rocks and out toward sea.

Whitecaps rolled in her wake and sunlight glinted off her silvery fins. I heard a roaring noise, and my heart jumped when I saw a speedboat appear from an outcropping of rocks.

I squinted in the distance, fear washing through me as I watched the boat zoom after Galena. A tall man stood at its helm, shouting orders. A large net was flung overboard and came down on Galena. Her hair and fins tangled as the net closed around her. With a tug, the net tightened and dragged the struggling mermaid into the boat.

There was a cheer from the boat and I got a good look at the tall man.

There was no mistaking his shaved head and swagger.

Mooncraft had captured his mermaid.

chapter thirty
# Cleaning Up

I wanted to forget about Galena. After all, what had she done for me? She had pretended to be my friend, stole my body, and left me to pay for her crimes. If she'd had her way, I would be the one snagged in a net. I didn't owe her anything. In fact, she was getting exactly what she deserved. I should be happy.

And I was happy to be back to normal. Ordinary brown hair, average shape, and knobby knees. Sure, I wore ridiculous jewelry and my mother's silk robe, but I was ME again. Even with a stinging sunburn, it felt wonderful!

But Stelleri was clearly upset. Despite everything, she cared about her cousin. "This is terrible. I better go tell my aunt."

"Can she help?"

"If she wants to."

"Can you meet me back here and let me know what happens?"

"All right. I'll return as the sun begins to set." She glanced at the sky the way I would check my watch. Then she waved and vanished underwater.

Lucas and I stood silently, watching the waves. The surf rolled in and out without any sign of a mermaid. I hoped Stelleri made it home safely.

A short time later, I was back at the hotel.

I wore jeans, sandals, and no jewelry (not even my watch). It was great to move on legs again. Kicking off my sandals and feeling soft carpet under my feet, I danced and twirled and laughed.

Lucas stayed at the hotel to study his lines (the real lines, not the fake ones he made up to fool Galena). I headed for the beach cleanup.

When Rosalie saw me coming, she raised her brows in question.

"Relax," I told her. "It's me."

"How can I be sure?"

"After your soccer coach, you had a crush on—"

"Okay!" She put up her hand. "I believe you . . . and I'm glad you're back. So tell me everything."

"Not now." I glanced around at the busy groups of volunteers picking up garbage from the beach. Later, when we were alone, I'd tell her about mermaids, aliens, and little people. Finally we'd have our talk.

Smiling to myself, I went over to Cleanup Central and found Mom.

"Cassie!" Her face lit up. "You did come!"

"How could I stay away?"

"That's not what you said last night."

"Sorry for being a brat," I told her. "I really do want to help with the cleanup. Just tell me where to start."

I joined Rosalie's work team. We picked up papers, bottles, cans, diapers, and soggy clothes. Disgusting! How could people be so messy? I was glad to do my small part to return the beach to its natural beauty.

As I lugged my second bag of garbage to the pile, I noticed two men in business suits talking at a picnic table. I heard one of them say, "Mermaid?" My heart jumped. Were they talking about Galena?

She deserved whatever happens to her. I told myself that I didn't care. So why did I duck behind the garbage can next to the two men?

Eavesdropping was wrong. I knew this from personal experience. Like the campout when I'd spied on Dad and ended up being chased by two scary dogs. Or when Dad's TV show did an interview with famous people who thought they'd been cloned. When I found out my FAVORITE pop singer was going to be on the show, I had to be there. Unfortunately, the singer's bodyguards didn't agree.

Did I listen when Dad warned me to stay away? Well, sure. But that didn't stop me from hiding in a guestroom cabinet. When I heard my idol's voice, I almost fainted. Then I heard him talk on the phone to his girlfriend, make an appointment to get another tattoo, and order lunch (pastrami on wheat, hold the mustard).

Listening to him talk about food made me hungry, which made my stomach growl, which gave me away. Oops!

After the bodyguards let me go, Dad gave me the big evils of eavesdropping lecture. He warned me that my curiosity would land me into deep trouble.

I hated it when Dad was right.

## chapter thirty-one

# Bad News

Crouched behind a stinky garbage can and half-buried in the sand, I'd heard plenty.

The men were reporters from an Oregon newspaper. They'd received a tip that Mooncraft had evidence that mermaids existed and he was going to give a press conference. They joked how this was probably another "Fiji Mermaid" hoax.

*Poor Galena!* I thought, surprised to feel sorry for someone who almost ruined my life. Despite a cramp in my leg and itches from sand fleas, I kept listening.

"I don't believe a word out of Mooncraft's lying mouth," the elder reporter said. "But I wouldn't miss a humdinger show like this for nothing."

"Me either," the younger reporter agreed. "Mooncraft must have something. Heard he hired security guards."

The elder guy snorted. "Must be to keep out snoops like us."

"Ain't that the truth? Well, we'll find out at eight."

*Eight tonight?* I jumped in surprise and smacked my knee into the garbage can.

"What was that?" the elder reporter asked and then I heard footsteps.

Oops! Trouble nipped at me like the sand fleas. Caught eavesdropping again!

Well, I wasn't sticking around for explanations. So I leapt up and took off running. I heard a shout, but kept going. When I returned to Rosalie, I was out of breath—but full of news.

When I told what I'd overheard, her dark eyes widened. "Wow! That will be some show."

"Yeah," I said, bending over to pick up an old sneaker. "Galena was terrible to me, but I never wanted anything this bad to happen. I feel sorry for her."

"Don't," Rosalie said firmly. "She played a mean game and deserves the results."

"Being on display like a zoo animal would be horrible."

"It's not your problem."

"I know . . ." I sighed. "It just feels wrong doing nothing."

"We're doing something. We're working hard to clean up the beach." Rosalie grinned and stabbed a candy wrapper with her pointed stick. "You're helping the environment. It's up to Galena's family to take care of her."

"They have magic," I said hopefully. "They'll figure out a way to free her."

But later, when I talked to Stelleri, I found out shocking news.

Rosalie covered for me with my parents while I went back to the cove to meet with Stelleri. She was waiting for me. Her eyes were red and her cheeks streaked with tears.

"Oh, Cassie!" she sobbed.

"What happened?"

"The council had a meeting and it's terrible!" Stelleri held onto a rock with one hand and wiped her tears with the other. "They . . . they voted not to save Galena!"

"Why not?" I exclaimed.

"Too many humans are involved. They won't risk the entire community for a law-breaking mermaid."

"But if they do nothing, Mooncraft will prove they exist. People will search the oceans for more mermaids once they see Galena on TV."

"Galena won't be seen." Stelleri glanced away uneasily.

"Of course she will. Mooncraft plans to reveal her to the media tonight, which means she'll be broadcasted all over the world."

"It won't happen." Her voice broke and she started to cry.

"What do you mean?" I waded into the chilly water and put my arms around her. "I don't understand."

"That's because you," she sniffled, "you don't know what happens to a mermaid when she's away from the ocean for too long."

I swallowed hard. "Tell me."

"Mermaids can't live in captivity. She probably has another hour or two . . . then it will be too late."

"She'll die?" I choked out in horror.

"Worse than death. Her life force will fade away and her body will shrivel until there's nothing left but scales and twisted bones."

"NO!" A wave slapped my legs, nearly knocking me over. "That can't be true!"

"But it is. By tonight, instead of Galena the beautiful mermaid, people will see a hideous skeleton."

I thought of the Fiji Mermaid I'd seen in the museum. Everyone assumed the hideous skeleton was a fake. But what if they were wrong? Had the monstrous Fiji Mermaid been a real mermaid at one time?

Is that what would happen to Galena?

Would she become a Fiji Mermaid, too?

## chapter thirty-two

# Conning a Con Man

If Galena's family wouldn't save her with magic, what could I do? Coming up with a plan to get my body back from Galena hadn't been too hard. But fooling a professional con man like Mooncraft would be almost impossible.

Still, Stelleri and I talked things over and came up with a plan. Then we parted and I headed back to the hotel.

When I entered my room, I saw the connecting door open and smelled something yummy. Mom had ordered in vegetarian pizzas.

"I'm sorry we're aren't going out to dinner like we planned," she apologized.

This was news to me since I'd been dining on sea plants and hadn't been around. Pizza looked good to me. My stomach grumbled and I grabbed a steamy slice. As I chewed, I waited for my parents to leave. Then I could send Amber to the bathroom to feed her sea monkeys and talk privately to Rosalie and Lucas.

So I was pleased when my parents headed for the door.

"You kids watch TV and enjoy your dinner," Mom said. "If you need us, we'll be at the Royal Crowne Hotel."

"Royal Crowne!" I almost choked on my pizza. "Why are you going there?"

"For a comedy show." Mom chuckled.

"It's sure to be hilarious." Dad slipped his arm over her shoulders. "Watching my competitor make a fool of himself."

"You . . . you mean Mooncraft?" I stammered.

"The one and only." Dad grinned. "Have fun kids—I know I will."

The thud of the shutting door echoed a warning in my head.

Once I explained the plan to Rosalie and Lucas, they agreed to help. But I was more worried than ever. Sneaking around the Royal Crowne Hotel would be hard enough with security guards. Now we had to avoid Mom and Dad, too.

Not only that—but we also had to take Amber.

And typical Amber—she insisted on bringing her sea monkeys. She kept them hidden in a bag. "Don't tell anyone," she whispered. "You promised."

I reminded her that she'd made a promise to me, too, and had to do whatever I told her. It was a deal.

We waited until seven o'clock, then headed over to the Royal Crown Hotel.

While Rosalie and Lucas (with Amber, too) searched the hotel for Galena, I went after Mooncraft.

I found him in the lobby, holding court with a few reporters. I'd seen him on TV, but never up close. He was really tall, over six-five, and wore a formal black suit and yellow tie. He had heavy eyebrows, a shaved head, and a gold hoop in one ear. Sort of a cross between a basketball star and a pirate.

He excused himself from the group, saying he'd see them soon in the conference room. Once he started down a hallway, I hurried after him.

"Mr. Mooncraft," I called out.

He turned, then paused a moment to size me up. Apparently being half his size made me half as interesting. "I don't have time for autographs."

"That's not why I'm here!" I took a deep breath. "I saw something in the ocean that I thought was a big fish. Only it was a person with a tail! I heard you knew about that kind of thing so I came right here to tell you."

Now I had his interest. His dark brows arched to sharp points as he leaned closer to me. "You saw a mermaid?"

I pretended to be confused. "I—I don't know. He wasn't a girl . . ."

"A merman!"

"I'll show you where," I offered.

I couldn't give him time to think or call for his employees. So I turned around and took off running. Naturally, he followed.

It was just a short jog to the beach. Mooncraft caught up with me.

"Where did you see him?" he asked, the setting sun glinting off his gold earring.

"Over there." I pointed to the cove.

I crossed my fingers and hoped that Stelleri was able to convince Astor to help. When I saw a flash of silver-green, I knew she'd succeeded.

"Oh my! Another mermaid!" Mooncraft cried out in delight.

"Merguy," I corrected. But he didn't hear because he was already running toward Astor.

"I have to catch him! Not only will I be the most famous man in the world, but I'll get a million from that moron Strange."

I gritted my teeth so I wouldn't lose my temper. Dad's TV show offered a million dollars to anyone who could prove something supernatural existed. I would rather eat sand than see the prize go to Mooncraft.

"I must have the merman!" Mooncraft turned to me. "Little girl, this is very important. Go back to the hotel and find a man named Kolby Dare. Tell him—and no one else—about the merman."

"How will I find him?" I asked innocently.

"Ask someone at the front desk. Just hurry! I can't lose my treasure!"

*Oh, you'll lose more than that,* I thought with a secret smile. *Stelleri and Astor will make sure of it.*

Then I crossed my fingers and headed back to the hotel.

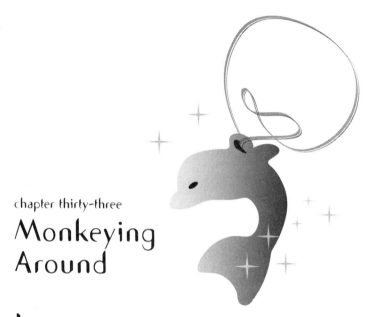

chapter thirty-three

# Monkeying Around

I waited behind the back door of the conference room. Tapping my fingers on the wall, I checked the time again. Almost 7:50. Where were they?

The audience was getting restless, too. I'd peaked in a few times and spotted my parents in the second row. I noticed that Dad's photographer, Fred, was there, too, with his camera.

But I'd been waiting for over twenty minutes and no sign of Lucas, Rosalie, and Amber. Had they been successful?

I was ready to go look for them when I heard a "psst!"

"Thank goodness!" I exclaimed in relief. Lucas, Rosalie, and Amber came beside me. Amber was the only one not smiling. "You found her?" I asked.

"Yeah." Lucas nodded. "Then we gave the guards your note."

"How many guards?" I asked.

"Two."

"Is that all?" I had expected at least five guards. But then Mooncraft was known for exaggeration. "Were they suspicious?"

"Not after we told them we were Mooncraft's kids."

I laughed. Leave it to Lucas to add more drama.

"I never knew you were so good at faking notes. It could come in handy when school starts," Rosalie joked. "Think you can do my mom's signature?"

"Nope. The only reason I tried it this time was because I knew the guards were hired today. So they wouldn't know Mooncraft's handwriting."

"Good thinking." Rosalie high-fived me.

"What did you write?" Lucas asked.

"To leave immediately to meet Mooncraft on the beach and their paychecks would be doubled." I paused, biting my lip. "Once the guards were gone, did you find Galena?"

"Yeah. She was in a big tank behind a stage curtain and she looked sick. Her skin was all wrinkly, and she weighed less than Amber. Rosalie wrapped her in a blanket and we carried her through a back door and out to the ocean."

"Far away from the cove," Rosalie added.

Amber folded her arms. "I was cold and you walked too fast."

"Don't mind her," Rosalie said with a wave of her hand. "She's in a bad mood."

"I want to go back," Amber pouted.

"Amber," I said firmly, "remember you promised to be good."

"But you don't know . . . I have to tell you—"

"It can wait, Amber."

"But Cassie!" She stomped her feet.

Ignoring my sister, I turned back to Rosalie and Lucas. "What about Galena? Did she make it to the ocean?"

"Not right away." My brother chuckled. "That other mermaid showed up."

"Stelleri?" I asked, a bit surprised. I figured Stelleri would stay far away from the shore once she and Astor had delayed Mooncraft.

"Yeah. She asked me to sit Galena in the water, but not to let her go until she reversed a spell. Something to do with a smile."

"Did it work?" I asked eagerly.

"I think so. When Galena hit the water, her skin and hair got better. But she was still weak and didn't have the energy to argue with her cousin. So she rubbed her bracelet—it looked like a dolphin again—and chanted a poem. She looked really angry when it was over, but Stelleri was grinning."

"Stelleri will be smiling a lot more now," I said with a smile of my own. "But I'm not so sure about Galena."

"Galena is back to her usual snooty self," Rosalie added. "After all our work, she just swam away. She never even said thank-you."

*Galena will never change,* I thought wryly. *But thank goodness I have—and Stelleri, too.*

\* \* \*

When Mooncraft showed up fifteen minutes late, his black suit was drenched and seaweed clung to his shoes. But he smiled coolly and apologized for the delay. He spent about ten minutes talking about how great he was, and then he announced that he would reveal his "astonishing discovery that would shock the world."

The room went quiet.

From the doorway in the far back, I could see a stage covered with a curtain. Someone put on music, and then the curtain slowly rolled up. The music grew louder and the audience hushed.

A large tank sat in the center of the stage. Mooncraft gave the signal and a spotlight shone on the tub. He proudly strutted over, his arm out as he gestured to his "discovery."

Only when he looked in the tank, his face went pale.

"WHERE IS SHE!" he thundered. "And what is THIS?"

He reached on a table beside the tank and lifted up a familiar plastic bowl.

Beside me, Amber jumped up and screamed, "My babies! Give them back!"

Then my little sister rushed up to the stage to rescue her sea monkeys.

chapter thirty-four
# Best Secrets

"I should have realized Amber didn't have her bag with sea monkeys. She must have lost them when you rescued Galena. No wonder she was cranky," I told Rosalie late that night when all the excitement died down. We were lounging in our pajamas and the lights were out. But we were too excited to sleep.

"Your parents were so shocked to see us there."

"Yeah. But they were laughing too hard to get really mad."

"I didn't even know she had sea monkeys."

"It was our secret."

"Well nothing is a secret anymore," Rosalie said with a giggle.

"Except mermaids," I added happily. "Now that it's all over, I have to admit it was all thrilling—swimming underwater, seeing odd creatures, and meeting mer-people. You should see their homes—they call them dwellings—they live in these towering caves."

"How cool!"

"They have this energy source called Heartlight and these giant extinct sea creatures. I was scared a lot, but I had fun too, like when I rode a dolphin."

"Wow!" Her eyes widened. "What was it like?"

"Like flying on waves. It was amazing."

"I wish I could have been there."

"Me, too." I paused, then added, "I'm sorry for being such a jerk about Georgia. I was just jealous I guess."

"It's okay. She's a cool friend, but not my *best* friend."

"Stelleri was a cool friend, too."

"Do you think you'll ever see her again?"

"I hope so." I hugged my pillow and thought of other friends I wanted to see again, like Vee, Maristella, and Hank. "Rosalie, there's more I have to tell you."

Then with Amber snoring across the room, I shared my best secrets with my best friend.

* * *

The last morning in Newport began with a lecture from Dad about leaving the hotel room without permission. Then we went out to breakfast.

Everyone was in great spirits.

Dad would add the footage of Mooncraft unveiling his "mermaid" to his "Famous Fakes" show. He'd end with his trademark line, "And that's why *I* don't believe it!" Mom's beach cleanup had been a success, and she was already planning the next one. Rosalie's team had won the volleyball game, and she couldn't wait to tell her family. Lucas had his lines memorized and would star in his first play next week. And Amber was the proud mommy of tiny, wiggly sea monkeys.

I was feeling good, too. My trip hadn't turned out like I expected, but it had sure been exciting. And this time Rosalie shared in the adventure.

Still, I was ready to go back home and had my bag packed before anyone.

So while everyone else was packing, I went downstairs to turn in my room key.

But after dropping off the key and turning down a narrow hall, a tall, shaved-headed man blocked my way: Sebastian Mooncraft.

Before I could cry out, he grabbed my arm. "Just a minute, little girl."

"Let me go!"

"Not until we've had a talk." His brows arched like devil horns as he bent down toward me. "You stole my mermaid and made a laughing stock out of me."

"I don't know what you're talking about."

"Yes you do! I didn't recognize you at first, but then I realized you were Strange's daughter."

"You better let me go. Dad will be down any minute." I glanced over at the elevator, willing it to open.

"He planned this, didn't he? Well, you can tell him—"

I jerked my arm and started to run away. He grabbed for me, but caught my jacket pocket. Tugging hard, I heard nylon rip. My pocket tore and I heard something fall on the carpet.

Instead of running, I reached down—but Mooncraft was quicker.

He picked up my crystal globe. "What's this?"

I froze. Panic raced through me. What if he saw images inside?

I relaxed a little when the globe remained gray and ordinary. Away from magic, it was no more than a pretty stone.

"That's mine," I demanded in a shaky voice.

He twirled it slowly between his fingers, saying nothing.

"Give it back. Please," I added desperately.

"Why?" He regarded me suspiciously. "What's so special about this crystal?"

"Nothing. It's just pretty and I like it."

"Since you took something from me, it's only fair I take something from you." He scowled. "But not this worthless rock."

He threw the crystal back to me.

I caught it and hugged it to my pounding chest.

"You and your father owe me—and I will get my revenge." He narrowed his gaze and added in a low threat, "Next time."

Then he turned and strode away.

But I had a sick feeling I hadn't seen the last of him.

I'd made a dangerous enemy in Sebastian Mooncraft.

The End

If you liked Strange Encounters, you'll love Linda Joy Singleton's young adult series, The Seer. The following excerpt from *Don't Die Dragonfly* should get your spine tingling and your senses swirling. Intended for ages 12 and up, Linda Joy Singleton's tantalizing series is sure to leave you breathless!

Make sure to log on to **http://teen.llewellyn.com** and get your own copies today! If you're under 18, make sure to get your parent's permission.

---

Everything about Sabine is normal, except for one thing—she can see the future. When she gets a vision of a girl with a dragonfly tattoo, she knows immediately that the girl is going to die. In order to stop a tragedy, Sabine must find out who the girl is, find a way to save her, and protect her psychic secret before someone gets hurt.

# WHAT'S UP THIS WEEK

### Psychic advice from
### Mystic Manny Devries

Romantics, listen up! Hold your heart tight. Beware of false promises and fake jewelry.

Green is the lucky color of the week. (Could some unexpected money be coming your way?)

Lucky numbers for this week are 8 and 11.

A kind act will result in many surprising opportunities.

And, to the girl with a dragonfly tattoo, don't do it . . .

# FOOTBALL TEAM READY TO RUMBLE

by Vic Wind

Sheridan High's varsity football team began practices yesterday amid rumors about the presence of Pac 10 scouts at the big game with Waindale Central High next month.

# TEACHE

by Dolores Haze

When faced the problem
brow for two eyes, any
would reach for tweezers,

Apparently not all mem
trious staff of Sheridan V.
the same instincts as the
tain chemistry teacher w
nameless is a principal off

"I mean, how can I be ex
trate on what he's saying
whatever when there's a ca
out on his forehead?"
Megan Atwood.

Sebastian Knight, a j
that perhaps someone
creetly slip this teacher
like, maybe he just doesr

Other students worry
grooming is an incurabl
ondary school faculty, ar
not be any hope..

Jerome Dunn said,
there was this calculu
feet were so bad that w
was coming down the
utes before he came i
him but he didn't beli

"Don't do what?" Manny's beaded dreadlocks rattled as he turned from his computer screen to face me. "Sabine, is this dragonfly girl for real?"

"Of course not." My heart pounded, but I kept my voice calm as I glanced up from the article I was proofreading. School had ended, and except for our teacher, we were the only ones left in the computer lab. "You asked for prediction suggestions and I made up some. If you don't like my ideas, come up with your own."

"It's just a weird thing to say—even for my Mystic Manny column."

"Use it or don't. Whatever." I leaned forward so my blond hair fell, partially concealing my face. If Manny discovered my secret, everything would be ruined.

"Help me here, okay?" He held out his hands. "My column goes to press in thirty minutes."

"Use your psychic powers to figure it out."

"Yeah, right." He snorted. "I don't believe that crap any more than you do."

I gripped my red pencil tightly. "But your readers believe."

"Nah, most of them know it's just a big joke. 'Manny the Mystic knows all and tells all.' Ha! If I could predict the future, you think I'd waste my time at school? No way! I'd pick lottery numbers and predict a sunny future of wealth, women, and tropical beaches."

"Get over yourself already." I checked my watch. "And you have just twenty-seven minutes till deadline."

"Beany, you're one cruel girl."

"Coming from you, I'll take it as a compliment. And don't call me Beany."

"Most girls would be flattered if I gave them a nickname."

"I'm not most girls. And you have twenty-six minutes now." I flipped through last week's edition of the *Sheridan Shout-Out*. My job was copy editor, not columnist. Working on commas and misspelled words suited my new image: helpful and orderly. After my problems at my last school, it was a huge relief to blend in like I was normal. And being on the newspaper made me part of Sheridan High's "In Crowd" without having to reveal much about myself—a great arrangement I wasn't about to risk. Next time Manny asked for help, I'd shout out a big "NO!"

But Manny didn't give up so easily. He pushed his dreads back from his forehead and then scrunched up his face into a pitiful expression. "Come on, Sabine. You have the best ideas. The part about a girl with a dragonfly tattoo—genius. Really, it's a great image—my readers will eat it up. But I can't just say 'Don't do it' without knowing what 'it' is."

*It. It. It.* The word pounded like a headache and I felt that familiar dizziness. Vivid colors flashed in my head: crimson red swirling with neon black. And I heard a wild flapping of wings. Warning of danger.

Not again, I thought anxiously. I hadn't had a vision since moving to Sheridan Valley, and I'd figured I was through with the weirdness. No longer the freak who knew things before they happened yet had no power to change them.

The dizziness worsened, and I fought for control. Stumbling, I grabbed the edge of a table so I wouldn't fall.

From faraway I heard Manny's voice asking what was wrong; then the lights in the classroom flickered and the drone of computers faded to a distant buzz.

Everything was dark, as if I were swimming in a murky sea at night. Then a light sparked and grew brighter and brighter, taking the shape of a girl. She was stunning, with waves of jet-black hair and olive skin that glistened like sea mist.

She lifted her hand to the sky, and a tiny purple-black creature with iridescent wings and quivering antennae fluttered to her wrist. A dragonfly. She smiled and caressed the wings. But her smile froze in horror as the creature changed, becoming a fanged monster that sank its sharp teeth into her smooth skin. Blood spurted, swelling like a tide. The girl opened her mouth to cry for help, but there only came a rush of crimson waves, and then she sank out of sight.

No, no! I tried to scream. But I was helpless to save her, caught in a dark current of despair that pulled me down, down, into a pool of blood.

✗     ✗     ✗

"HEY, BEANY?"

Gasping for breath, I blinked and saw Manny's black eyes staring at me with concern. The dizziness passed and my head cleared. "Huh?" I murmured.

"Are you sick or something?" he asked.

Lights grew bright again and I realized I was still clutching the table. I relaxed my grip. "I'm fine."

Manny gently touched my shoulder. "You don't look fine. What's wrong?"

"Nothing. Just tired." My breath came fast.

"But you're all trembling."

"Guess that test in calculus wiped me out." I managed a shaky laugh. "I– I just remembered someplace I have to go."

"But Beany—"

"Sorry! Talk to you later."

Then I fled—running as if flocks of winged demons chased after me.

✗     ✗     ✗

BY THE TIME I MADE A SHARP LEFT ON LILAC LANE, AN UNPAVED, rutted road, the dark images had faded. Still, I was left with a stark fear.

When I slipped through the iron gate of Nona's driveway, my fears eased. The weathered yellow house had been my touchstone since I was

235

little, a haven where nothing could get me. I loved Nona's cozy farmhouse, with its big wraparound porch, rambling red barn, cows, goats, horses, chickens, dogs, and cats.

Ten acres of tangled woods stretched far behind the pasture, bumping up against new developments. Sheridan Valley used to be a quiet farming town, but its central location made it an easy commute to Stockton or Sacramento, and the population had skyrocketed. Still, it maintained a slow pace and country charm, and I'd been truly happy since moving here. Even with upscale houses squeezing in from both sides, Nona's home was my paradise.

And there was Nona. Crouched on her knees in the garden, a wide-brimmed straw hat shading her deep-lined face. She'd done so much for me: taking me in when my parents sent me away, holding me tight to heal the hidden hurts.

Watching her tend her garden, I longed to rush into her comforting arms. She knew all about visions and predictions. She would understand my anxiety more than anyone. But I couldn't confide in her—because of the lie.

Sighing, I avoided Nona by doubling around to the back of the house. Since there was no one I could talk to, I'd purge my demons with loud music and a bath of scented bubbles.

As I hurried up the wooden steps, chickens squawked out of my way, and a white cat with mismatched eyes regarded me solemnly.

"Don't give me that look, Lilybelle. I've had a bad day and I don't need any of your attitude." I patted her silky fur and pushed open the screen door.

There was an odd scent in the air—musty and a little wild. As I made my way through the laundry room and kitchen, I tried to identify the unfamiliar odor. It reminded me of a sunny morning after a summer storm. Fresh, light, but also a little sultry. Had Nona concocted a new herbal carpet freshener? She only used natural cleaners and remedies like crushed pine needle shampoo, goat's milk soap, and a honey rose-petal elixir for sore throats. The smell grew stronger as I walked down the narrow hall, which was decorated with family pictures: Mom as a baby, my parents on their wedding day, and portraits of Nona's three deceased husbands.

A sloshing sound stopped me cold.

From the bathroom. But that wasn't possible. Nona and I lived alone.

I started down the hall, but then doubled back to the kitchen to grab a broom—not that I'd need a weapon, but it wouldn't hurt. Holding it out in front of me like a sword, I moved cautiously down the hall. The bathroom door was open a crack, and through it I could see the sink, filled to the top with water. And perched on the silver faucet was a large bird. A falcon! Why was a falcon taking a bath in my sink?

But the bird wasn't alone.

When I saw the shadowy figure by the hamper, I was so startled I dropped my broom. The bird screeched and ruffled its powerful wings. Before I could scream, the shadowed person lunged for me. He slapped one arm across my shoulders and clamped down over my mouth with the other hand.

"Shush!" he ordered in a harsh whisper. "Don't make a sound."

I struggled, hitting and jabbing with my elbows. But his grip was firm. He dragged me away from the bathroom. My shock switched to anger. How dare this guy attack me in my own home! I kicked him in the leg as hard as I could.

He grunted with pain. "Cut it out!" he cried.

I kicked again, and when he jerked back, his hand over my mouth loosened, so I bit down. Hard.

"HEY! That hurt!"

"Good!" I squirmed and slipped out of his grasp. "I hope I drew blood."

"Geez, you bite worse than a badger." He sucked his injured hand. "Nona was way off when she told me about you."

I backed against a wall. "You know my grandmother?"

"Why else would I be here?"

"You tell me! And what's with the bird?" Hugging myself, I stared, really seeing him for the first time. He was youngish, maybe seventeen or eighteen. He was a few inches taller than I was, maybe five-foot-ten. He was wiry, with muscular arms, sandy-brown hair, and eyes like silver-blue mirrors. His jeans were dark, and he wore an unbuttoned, brown flannel shirt over a faded blue T-shirt.

"He's a falcon, and he got oil on his wings, so I brought him inside to clean up. Sorry if I scared you," he said.

"I wasn't scared."

"I didn't want you to startle Dagger." He glanced toward the bathroom where I heard a soft swish of water.

"You *own* a falcon?"

"Wild creatures can't be owned. But he trusts me. If you'd screamed, he would have panicked and hurt himself. Hey, relax. I'm not going to attack you."

"Oh, thanks," I said sarcastically. "I am so reassured. What do you call what just happened? A friendly handshake?"

"Hey, I'm the one bleeding." He held out his hand, where a reddish half circle of teeth marks contrasted his tanned skin. Blood trickled from the deepest mark.

I ignored his hand and gave him a sizzling look. "Explain yourself," I demanded. "What are you doing here?"

"I invited him."

Whirling around, I saw Nona. She still wore her wide-brimmed straw hat, and there was a smudge of dirt on her cheek.

"You– You did?" I stammered. "But why?"

"Dominic is going to stay here to help with repairs and care for the animals."

"Why hire someone? I can help you."

"Not in the way he can. So stop scowling and welcome him, Sabine." Nona smiled. "Dominic is part of our family now."

*　　*　　*

AFTER SLAMMING THE DOOR TO MY ROOM, I SORTED THROUGH MY CDs looking for something to match my mood.

If I were at school, I'd listen to the trendy artists everyone raved about. But at home, I could be myself, giving into my secret passion for eclectic music. I indulged in music the same way some people ate certain foods for emotional comfort. Classical for introspective moments, jazz for happy times, and heavy metal for dark, furious moods.

But not even the pounding sound of Metallica and rose-scented bubbles could calm me. How could Nona invite a stranger to live with us without even asking me? It wasn't right! Nona and I had settled into a comfortable routine and got along great. We didn't need anyone else. Not my parents or neighbors—and definitely not some weird guy with a falcon.

I held my breath and sank deep under the warm water.

*Stop feeling sorry for yourself,* a voice said.

"Go away, Opal," I replied with my thoughts. "I have enough problems."

*You don't know how good you have it. When I was your age—*

"Not one of your My-Life-Was-Torture stories." I couldn't hold my breath anymore and came up for air. Music vibrated the walls, but the voice in my head came through louder. With my eyes still closed, I could see Opal's critical arched brows and dark eyes. For a spirit guide, she was a terrible nag.

*You were rude to that young man,* she complained. *Didn't I teach you better manners than that? He's important, you know—or you would know if you listened instead of being so stubborn.*

"Stay out of my head," I told her. "I'm normal now. I have a cool best friend who is even a cheerleader; I'm on the school newspaper staff; and kids like me because I don't hear voices, see spirits, or predict death. No one knows what happened at my other school. I've started over, and I don't want you to interfere."

*Whine, whine, whine. You can't run from who you are, so why fight it?*

"Go away." I sloshed out of the tub, grabbed a towel, and snapped off the CD.

After I was dressed, I climbed up a curved staircase to my bedroom. It used to be an attic until four months ago when I moved in. Nona had offered me the guestroom next to her office, but I'd begged for the cozy attic room, with its arched ceiling and view of the woods.

Nona also gave me free rein to decorate my room. I chose a lavender theme, draping silky fabric around the windows and arranging daisy-shaped rugs on the polished wood floor. Along with my taste in music, I had "different" taste in hobbies. I'd had recently started embroidering a pillow to match my white and purple quilted comforter. I kept my craft materials in a cedar trunk that used to belong to Nona's mother.

Working with my hands always relaxed me, so I slid open the trunk and pulled out the pillow. Using yarn shades from snow white to pale lavender, I'd already embroidered half of the winter landscape picture. At first glance, the soft threads were all white. But as you peered closer, shapes clarified—an owl, a snowman, hills, trees, and a snow-covered cottage.

Weaving my needle in and out, I leaned against the cushion in my window seat and stared across the tops of lush green pines. It was great here at Nona's and I'd never been happier. So why did Nona have to spoil everything by inviting him?

"It's just not right," I complained to my best friend the next day at school. "He's not even friendly. After that whole mess in the bathroom, he's avoided me."

"Maybe he's shy," Penny Lovell—nicknamed Penny-Love—said as she slammed her locker shut. We met every morning at our lockers and caught up on the latest gossip. Bright as sunshine with curly copper-red hair, Penny-Love spun the social wheels around school, and usually did all the talking. But today I had plenty to say.

"His only excuse is a bad attitude. Yet the way Nona treats him, you'd think he was royalty. He doesn't bother coming in to dinner; Nona takes a tray out to him—like she works for him, not the other way around."

"Your grandmother is only being kind."

"This is beyond normal kindness. She gave him the barn apartment, which is bigger than my room and has electricity and a private bathroom. And Nona says she's going to get him a small refrigerator. Can you believe it?"

Penny-Love paused to wave at a group of girls passing by. Then she turned back to me. "Uh, sure. But you haven't told me the important details. Like what he *looks* like."

"He's just weird." I frowned. "There's something strange about him. I can't figure out what exactly; it's just a feeling I have."

Penny-Love giggled. "Maybe you should ask Manny the Mystic for advice. Did you see his column yet?"

"Is it out already?"

"Yeah. And it's better than usual. Here." She unzipped a pocket of her backpack and withdrew a folded newspaper. "Check it out."

My fingers trembled slightly as I unfolded the paper. A dragonfly with bloody wings flashed in my mind. I shut out the image and focused on the paper.

Penny-Love was right—Manny had outdone himself. He'd added a "spotlight on the future" feature where he picked a random student and predicted her life ten years from now. Sophomore Amanda Redmond was destined to have a great career as a fashion designer, marry an airplane pilot, and have three children—all boys.

Reading over my shoulder, Penny-Love chuckled. "Amanda? A fashion designer? That'll be the day."

"How come?" I asked.

"She wears faded army fatigues and oversized hiking boots. She has zero fashion sense."

I thought Penny-Love was being kind of harsh, but our friendship was still new, so I didn't say anything.

Returning my gaze to the newspaper, I skimmed over the next predictions. Some of them were my suggestions, like the lucky color. Glancing down at the vines embroidered up the leg of my jeans, I hoped green would indeed prove lucky.

When I reached the end of the column and found no mention of the girl with a dragonfly tattoo, I felt relieved—and disappointed. I was glad my silly idea wasn't in print for everyone to see. But I felt uneasy, too, as if I'd let someone down.

"Cool, huh?" Penny-Love said as we reached our homeroom class. "I mean, I don't believe it or whatever, but it's fun. Where does Manny get all his ideas?"

"He has a good imagination. If he doesn't get that Pulitzer he's always talking about, he'll make a great tabloid writer."

"Is that a prediction?" she teased.

"No!" I said a bit too sharply. "I only believe facts."

"Like the fact that you're hot for Josh." She nudged me and pointed to a dark-haired boy as we took our seats. "You ever gonna tell him how you feel?"

My gaze drifted across desktops. The room suddenly felt warm and I couldn't stop staring. Josh DeMarco. Student council junior president, A+ student, a dedicated volunteer, and so fine that my heart sped up just being near him. He was too good to be true—maybe too good for me. And I hadn't found the nerve to talk to him. I probably never would.

The morning went by quickly with a surprise quiz in English lit and extra homework in Spanish. I always ate lunch in the cafeteria with Penny-Love and her group of cheerleading friends, but I'd forgotten my calculus book, so I made a detour to my locker. As I grabbed my book, out of the corner of my eye I glimpsed dark hair and a smile so sweet it took my breath away.

Josh.

Waving as he left his friends Zach and Evan, Josh was walking this way. In seconds, he'd pass by, just inches from me. This was my chance to talk to him, find out if he knew my name and might want to know more. Yeah, like that was going to happen! If I managed to utter one word that would be a miracle.

But I couldn't let him catch me staring, so I leaned closer to my locker—too close! I banged my head on the door, then lost my grip on my book, and it went crashing to the floor. By the time I'd picked it up and shut my locker, Josh had passed.

With a low groan, I watched him pause to talk to a girl with long brown hair, then laugh at something she said before continuing on his way.

243

Sounds faded and a fog rolled through my mind, clouding everything except Josh. It was as if I was standing next to him, moving in step and sharing his heartbeat. I could even hear this thoughts. He was thinking about his car—a secondhand Honda Civic—and planning to stop by an auto parts store after school to repair a broken taillight. Not paying attention, he walked into his auto shop class. I smelled grease and saw the instructor helping a skinny boy move a car on a lift.

Josh headed straight for a tool cabinet, crouching low to sort through a bottom drawer. He was directly in front of the lift, with his back to it.

My mind was still with Josh as I closed my own locker and began walking towards the auto shop, just at the end of the hallway.

I entered the classroom that was just outside the actual shop. A couple kids noticed me; one was a girl from my calc class.

"Hey, Sabine," she said, but I didn't say anything.

Josh was still hunched over the drawer, looking for something. "Spark plug gapping tool," I heard in my mind. The skinny boy had the control for the lift in his hand now, but the instructor had turned to help someone else.

I was standing in the doorway to the shop, just a few quick strides from Josh. I took a small step toward him.

There was a loud grinding noise and sparks from a machine on the other side of the shop. Josh was still searching. He had no idea. The boy at the lift timidly pushed a green button on the control. The wheels weren't secure; I just knew that. The noise was so loud, but I could somehow hear in Josh's head, "Where is that stupid thing?"

Suddenly, there was a jarring noise and one of the wheels slipped off the platform. The skinny boy frantically pushed the red button, but the car slipped forward. I was now moving in large strides toward Josh. There was so much noise! Running, I reached Josh and pushed him, hard, and we both tumbled over as the car came all the way off the lift and rolled forward, smashing into the tool cabinet where Josh had been standing.

The noise stopped. Josh looked at me. Everyone looked at me.

"Huh?" Josh said in bewilderment. "What just happened?"

Brushing dirt off my jeans, I stood up on shaky legs. I couldn't say anything because all the breath had been knocked out of me.

He smoothed back his dark hair, standing tall so he towered at least a head over me. "Do I know you?" he asked.

"Uh . . . well . . ." There goes Miss Conversationalist!

Realization seemed to dawn on him as he looked at the smashed cabinet and the lopsided car. "WOW! That almost hit me! Unbelievable!"

I managed a weak nod.

The instructor rushed over, and, after quickly making sure Josh was okay, he called some students to help move the car.

I started to go, when Josh touched my arm. "Wait."

I waited.

He pushed his hair from his eyes as he studied me. "I don't understand exactly what happened, but I know I owe you a huge thanks."

"Well . . ." Being near him stole my thoughts.

"How did you know?"

"I– I uh . . ." I took a deep breath. "I heard the wheels slip."

His dark brows arched. "How could you? It was too noisy to hear anything."

"Everyone says I have unusually good hearing." Did I just say that?

"Lucky for me."

"It's the color green." I pointed at his shirt. "It's lucky."

Josh blinked like he hadn't a clue what I was talking about.

"Don't you read Mystic Manny? He has a weekly column and it's mega popular, so you must have heard about it," I babbled like a fool. Now that I was finally talking to my dream guy, I didn't want it to end.

245

"Oh, yeah. I know who you mean."

"Then you know Manny writes for the *Sheridan Shout-Out.*"

"Oh. The school paper. I was interviewed in it a few weeks ago."

"The September thirteenth issue." I didn't add that I'd clipped the article and tacked it to the bulletin board in my bedroom. I kept right on blathering, "In every issue Manny picks a lucky color and it's green this week. See, I'm even wearing green vines on my jeans."

"Nice design," he said.

Was he checking me out? Did he like what he saw? I was kind of skinny, not much on top, more like a twelve-year-old than a sixteen-year-old. But my face was okay and Penny-Love said my long blond hair was my best feature, that the ribbon of black streaking through my hair was cool. Still, I was unsure. Afraid Josh would take one look at me and run away.

But he wasn't leaving. He was smiling—in a way that made me feel warm inside.

"I've seen you around," he said. "In English."

I stared up into his dark brown eyes and nodded.

"Sabrina?"

"Sabine."

"And I'm Josh."

"I know."

His grin widened into dimples. "Guess I owe you a big thanks. If you didn't have such great hearing, I could have been, like, dead."

"Nah. Only a broken leg or two."

"But I'm all in one piece. I really owe you big-time." He paused. "There must be something I can do to pay you back—"

"No, no! You don't have to—"

"But I want to—want to get to know you."

"Well . . . that would be cool."

"Are you doing something later this week? Want to see a movie?"

Did I ever! Of course, I didn't say this; instead, I kept my dignity and answered simply, "Sure."

✗   ✗   ✗

A DATE!

Penny-Love nearly choked on her pom-poms when I told her. After school, the other cheerleaders crowded around and wanted to know all the details. I was reluctant to talk so much about myself, not comfortable as the center of attention. But they kept after me, so I gave in and enjoyed the rush of being almost popular. So different than how I was treated at my last school.

And I couldn't wait to tell my grandmother about Josh. Nona was the expert on romance. She ran an online dating service called Soul-Mate Matches. Totally high tech, using compatibility analysis charts and personal videos. Of course, her amazing success rate had little to do with technology—but her clients didn't know that.

Dumping my backpack on the living room floor, I looked for my grandmother. Only she wasn't in the kitchen or her office. The light on her answering machine blinked, as if asking, "Where's Nona?"

Good question.

Heading outside, I checked the garden, chicken pen, and pasture. All that remained was the barn.

I still resented Nona's hiring of Dominic, but not even that could get me down today. I was imagining my grandmother's excited reaction to my news as I peeked into the rambling red barn.

"Nona?" I called out.

No answer, but I caught the scent of burnt lavender. Curious, I pushed open the door. Sunlight cascaded down through a high window, shining gold on stacks of hay. My footsteps on loose hay were soft.

A calf, penned for its own safety because it was lame, mooed at the two barn cats who chased each other across a wood rail. I'd always loved this barn, the musty hay smells and all the animals, even the occasional scurrying rat.

My gaze drifted up a staircase, to the loft apartment. The room had been off limits when Nona's last husband was alive and used it as an art studio. I heard the murmur of voices through the closed door—my grandmother and Dominic. A clunk and a rolling sound piqued my curiosity. So I crept up the stairs. After some hesitation, I reached for the door. At my touch, it fell open a few inches.

My grandmother sat cross-legged on a round carpet across from Dominic. Candles flickered and lavender incense wafted a sweet trail toward the ceiling. Whispering, Nona held out a handful of small stones to Dominic. Sparkling crystals, amethyst, and jade. Stones for meditation and healing. The true tools of Nona's romantic trade.

But why was she showing precious stones to a stranger who'd been hired to repair the barn, feed the animals, and muck out stalls? I felt sick inside, knowing Nona was keeping something from me. A secret was almost the same as a lie. And I knew too well how one lie led to another and another.

Backing away, unnoticed, I fled.

It was childish to feel hurt, left out, like the last kid chosen for a team. But that's how I felt. The happy bubble that I'd floated home in had popped.

I slammed the door behind me as I entered the house, heading for the kitchen, where I poured a glass of milk and ripped open a bag of wheat chips. I had just put the milk away when the phone rang.

Instead of answering right away, I played a childhood game. Closing my eyes and concentrating hard, I tried to summon an image of the caller. Not my parents, I realized with relief. Someone younger, but neither Amy nor Ashley, my nine-year-old twin sisters. Someone older and not related. A dark-haired male . . .

"OHMYGOD!" I blurted out. I snatched up the phone before the fifth and final ring.

It was Josh, wanting to know if I would mind doubling on Friday with his friend Evan and his latest girlfriend. Yes, yes, yes! Anything you say, Josh.

And with one short, magical phone call, my happy bubble was back. For the rest of the evening, I mentally tuned into a channel where Josh starred in every show. I called Penny-Love and we talked forever, debating what I should wear on Friday and discussing how far to go on a first date.

"It's not like I've never been on a date before," I told her. "Although it'll be my first since moving here."

"Did you have a boyfriend at your old school?"

"A few," I said evasively, not wanting to get on the topic of my past. "Besides, I won't even be alone with Josh on a double date. I'll be lucky to get a kiss good night."

Penny-Love then proceeded to tell me in dishy detail about some of her very memorable goodbye kisses. We were still talking when Nona finally came in after dark. My grandmother didn't tell me what she'd been doing, and I didn't tell her about Josh.

When I got ready for bed, I chose a heart-shaped nightlight and hoped for sweet dreams of Josh. The dark had always scared me; so, childish as it was, I never slept without a nightlight. This led to a huge nightlight collection. Plug-in lights shaped like kittens, dolphins, rainbows, angels, butterflies, and a stained-glass flaming dragon.

Instead of hearts, though, I dreamed of dragons. Dragons chasing after me, blowing molten fire, their razor teeth white knives of death. I ran and ran, calling out to Josh to rescue me. And there he was, tall and handsome, grasping my hand. He protected me with a silver shield, dodging bursts of flame. We raced through a maze of spindly spines that became a giant dragon.

There was a loud flapping, and the dragon sprouted wings. Josh slipped and started to fall, only I lunged forward and grasped his hand. Holding on tight, we clung together as the dragon flew higher, higher, soaring into the unknown. Then the dragon changed, spines smoothing into silky feathers and fangs curving into a sharp beak. Soaring along on a strong breeze, we rode the giant bird. A falcon. When I looked at Josh, he was different, too. His dark hair grew longer and lighter, to a sandy-brown, and his eyes shone as blue as the sky. Dominic . . .

I sat bolt up in bed.

My heart revved and my hands were sweaty. Despite my nightlight's reassuring glow, the shadows around my room moved and breathed, and I sensed I wasn't alone.

I was never alone.

Climbing out of bed, I walked over to the wall and snapped on the light.

Then I slipped back under my covers and sank into a fitful, dreamless sleep.

*       *       *

THE NEXT MORNING WHEN I WENT TO MY LOCKER TO MEET PENNY-Love, instead I found Josh. And this was only the beginning of a perfect day.

Just like that, I was Josh's girl. Instead of sitting with the cheerleaders at lunch, Josh and I sat outside under a willow tree, sharing sandwiches and chips and talking. Mostly, I listened while he described his interest in magic. Not the kind of magic I'd avoided all my life, but entertaining magic tricks.

He was apprenticing to join a professional magician's organization. So secret, he couldn't reveal much, except that only the most respected, skilled magicians belonged. And his mentor, the Amazing Arturo, was rumored to be a distant cousin of Houdini.

"How'd you get interested in magic?" I asked, impressed that a popular guy like Josh had such an unusual hobby.

"Arty—the Amazing Arturo—showed me some tricks and I was hooked."

"How long have you known him?"

"Seven years." Josh hesitated, taking a sip of cola. "We met at Valley General Hospital where he was giving a show in the children's ward."

"What were doing you there? Were you sick?"

"Not me. My older brother." His tone had grown serious.

"What was wrong with him?"

"A car accident. He was in a coma for five months."

"I'm sorry. How is he now?"

"He didn't make it." Josh spoke calmly but I sensed deep loss and I regretted asking the question. "It's been a long time," he quickly added. "And because Arty noticed me hanging around the hospital with nothing to do, one thing led to another, and now I'm the one performing for sick kids."

"That's great of you."

"It's the kids who are great. And it's so cool to amaze them. Wait till you see my latest sleight-of-hand trick. You'll never guess how it's done."

"I wouldn't even try. I'd rather be mystified."

"Then you gotta watch me the next time I perform at the hospital. Will you come?"

"I'd love to." And I loved staring at his face, his soft lips, straight nose, and long, dark lashes. He was so perfect. And he liked me. Amazing.

Penny-Love came over that night, just one day from The Date, and searched through my closet for the right outfit. Unfortunately, all my clothes were wrong. So I broke down and admitted to my grandmother why I needed a new outfit. She had a million questions about Josh and was impressed when I told her about his volunteer work. Always a fan of romance, Nona gave me encouragement—and her credit card— then told me to have fun shopping.

We headed for Arden Fair Mall in Sacramento, about thirty miles away. Penny-Love borrowed a station wagon from one of her older brothers. Nick or Jeff or Dan—with a family as large as hers, all red-heads with freckles, who could keep them straight?

The perfect outfit was a dark-green skirt with a yellow Lyrca top. Penny-Love talked me into buying one of those pushup bras, which made me blush when I looked in the mirror. For the first time in my life, I had curves in the right places.

✗   ✗   ✗

When Friday night arrived, I breathlessly watched Josh walk up to my front door. I didn't need to be psychic to know my outfit was working a subtle magic. This was my moment and nothing could spoil it. Not even Dominic, whom I saw standing in the shadow of the porch, scowling as Josh opened his car door for me. What was his problem any-way? He'd barely spoken two sentences to me since we'd met, yet I had the weird feeling he disapproved of my going out.

"You look great," Josh said as we drove off to pick up his friends.

My cheeks warmed. "Uh . . . thanks."

"I'm glad you don't mind doubling with Evan and Danielle."

"It'll be fun." I smiled.

He smiled back.

252

I could tell he liked me, but then when I thought about it, I wasn't sure and wondered why a great guy like him would even notice me. Sure I'd rescued him, yet gratitude wasn't any basis for a relationship. We'd gotten along great so far, but would that change if he knew the truth about me?

There was an awkward stretch of quiet, and I tried to think of something interesting to say. I had to be careful not to reveal too much, yet I didn't want to bore him with topics like weather or homework.

Then I remembered some advice I'd heard Nona give to one of her clients. When in doubt about what to say, ask your date about himself.

"So Josh," I said, "tell me about yourself."

"What?"

"Anything." I shrugged. "Like do you have a pet?"

"A dog named Reginald."

"Do you call him Reggie for short?"

"Nothing short about my giant dog. We nicknamed him Horse."

I laughed. "What's your family like?"

"They're great. Mom's a realtor and Dad has some kind of management job at EDH Compu-Tech. They're always busy, so we have this terrific housekeeper who makes the best lasagna."

"Oooh. My favorite," I said, smacking my lips. "I used to make it for my little sisters."

"How old are they?"

"Nine."

"Both of them?"

"Amy and Ashley are twins," I explained. Then, because I suspected he was thinking of his brother, I purposely switched the subject and asked him about the couple who would be joining us soon.

"Evan and I have been friends since we were babies, practically," Josh said as he slowed for a stop sign. "He's a year older, and a fantastic athlete. Football, wrestling, baseball—you name it, he's good enough to go pro. As for Danielle, I only know what Evan's told me, that she's smart and pretty. Evan dates a lot so it's hard to keep up."

"Do you date a lot, too?" I asked, then wanted to slap my hand over my mouth.

"Hardly ever," he said firmly. "Evan's fixed me up a few times, but it never works out. He says I'm too picky. But I only want to be with someone I respect."

He took his right hand off the steering wheel, resting it inches from my arm. I could feel his energy without even touching, and it made me a little dizzy. In a good way.

Then we were slowing and parking in front of a ranch-style home. Two figures came down the steps. I recognized Evan's cocky grin and wide, muscular shoulders from the sports section of the *Sheridan Shout-Out*. His arm was draped around the tiny waist of a slim, raven-haired girl. While he moved with confident strides, she sort of glided like a shadow beside him. She looked familiar, although she wasn't in any of my classes, and I was sure we hadn't met before. The feeling of knowing her was strong, so I turned around for a better look.

Danielle flashed me a nervous smile as she climbed into the backseat with Evan. She had an exotic sort of beauty—smooth olive skin, a nose that was a bit long, and high cheekbones. Her strapless, navy-blue sheer top showed off ample curves that didn't need any extra help. I felt a stab of envy, wishing looking good came so easily to me.

Then I noticed the dark tattoo on her wrist.

A tiny outline of a winged insect.

A dragonfly tattoo.